Come to My Tomorrowland

Illustrated by
Jim Marsh

Come to My Tomorrowland
By Jesse Stuart

Edited and with an Introduction by
Jerry A. Herndon

Jesse Stuart Foundation
Ashland, Kentucky
2009

Come to My Tomorrowland

Book Design by Flexisoft

ISBN: 0-945084-55-2

Published by
Jesse Stuart Foundation
1645 Winchester Avenue
Ashland, Ky 41101
606.326-1667 • JSFBOOKS.com

Dedication

*Millard Buckner Byrne and Nancy Marie Weyrich Byrne
dedicate this book for our love of our children,
Michael, John and Laura and the blessings of our grandchildren,
Kevin Michael, Sean Edwards, Kathleen Marie,
Jackson Weyrich, and Jamisen Lynlee Byrne*

*Left to Right: Kathleen Marie
Byrne, Sean Edwards Byrne,
and Kevin Michael Byrne*

*Jackson Weyrich Byrne and
Jamisen Lynlee Byrne*

Introduction

Before the Salk and Sabin vaccines were developed in the 1950s, polio, or poliomyelitis, was a worldwide health problem. The disease crippled thousands of people throughout the world every year, and was often called infantile paralysis because its victims were usually children.

Americans suffered from this terrifying disease along with the rest of the world, and Jesse Stuart was well aware of the tragedy it brought to young people. *Come to My Tomorrowland* is his tribute to the faith and courage shown by young victims of polio.

By the time he wrote this book about Joy Burton and her pet fawn, Jesse Stuart had already achieved fame for his novels for adult readers, and he had also written a very successful novel for high school age youth, *Hie to the Hunters*, a celebration of the joys of a farm boy's life. It tells the story of the friendship of a town boy, Did Hargis, and Sparkie, a boy from a hill farm. Did never learns to spit tobacco juice in a bully's eye, as Sparkie does, but several months of farm life make him as tough as a hickory knot. Before he goes back home, he has learned to hunt and fish and plow corn, and he is a very self-reliant young man.

Following the success of *Hie to the Hunters*, Stuart began writing books for elementary school children. His first two are among the best books available for young readers of grades 3-7. These are *The Beatinest Boy* (1953), a celebration of a boy's love for his grandmother, and *A Penny's Worth of Character* (1954), a story of a boy's learning the value of truthfulness and honesty in dealing with other people.

By 1970, Stuart had published seven books for younger readers. All seven are written from a boy's point of view. His last junior book, *Come to My Tomorrowland*, was published in 1971, though it was written much earlier, in the autumn of 1957 and the following winter. He revised it in the fall of 1959.

Jesse wrote *Come to My Tomorrowland* for Jessica Jane, the Stuarts' only child, and dedicated the book to her. To make the story truly a girl's book, he made Joy Burton the central character. It is the only one of his eight junior books told from a girl's viewpoint.

In this story of Joy Burton and her pet deer, Stuart expresses his love for both animals and people. He had been a hunter and trapper in his youth (like Did and Sparkie in *Hie to the Hunters*), and had used the money he earned from trapping to buy his clothes and school books, but when he grew up, he stopped hunting and trapping. He preferred to make his farm in W-Hollow a wildlife preserve, and he did not allow hunting on his farm. This is still true today. The Stuart farm is now a nature preserve, owned and managed by the Kentucky Nature Preserves Commission.

Stuart's compassion for Joy Burton, a young girl crippled by polio, is very clear in this book. He also clearly admires her spunk and courage. He and his brothers and sisters were raised by parents who taught them to overcome difficulties, not give in to them, and this is the strength of character Stuart gives to Joy Burton.

Glennis Stuart Liles, Jesse's sister, has suggested that the story of Joy Burton and her pet deer may be based on circumstances in the life of Jesse's niece, Vivian Keeney. "Bibbie," as she was called by her family, had lost the sight of one eye to a tuberculosis infection, and her health was fragile. She was not expected to live to grow up.

One hard winter, while the Keeney family was living in a cabin on the ridge above Jesse and Naomi Stuart's home in W-Hollow, some wild dogs attacked their sheep. The dogs killed a ewe, leaving her lamb an orphan. Bibbie raised the lamb on a bottle, and named it "Annie."

Bibbie Keeney's courage and her love for her pet lamb touched her Uncle Jesse's heart. He may have had Bibbie and Annie in mind when he created the story of

Joy Burton and Snowball for school children.

Vivian "Bibbie" Keeney did grow up, and she earned two college degrees. Like Joy Burton in *Come to My Tomorrowland,* her courage and cheerfulness helped her face and overcome life's difficulties, and made her memorable in the lives of those who knew her. Bibbie lives on in the character of Joy Burton, whose adventures and courage will be exciting and inspirational for young readers today.

Dr. Jerry A. Herndon
Murray State University
Murray, Kentucky
March 23, 1995

Chapter One

In a secluded part of Greenwood County there is a valley of surprising beauty. It is where Shacklerun Creek flows into the Little Sandy River. Here giant beeches, tall poplars, black gums, and oaks grow in abundance beside the lazy, meandering waters. On either side of the creek are steep slopes from which cliffs protrude in irregular patterns. Some giant pine trees grow on these slopes among the hardwoods.

Joy Burton stopped suddenly on the path beneath the gnarled old trees, for on the slope above the path she saw something she had never seen before. She saw a small white animal standing on three legs, holding its left hind leg off the ground. It was standing near a large pine tree, just below the rock cliff. The slender animal moved its pretty head. It held its nose high and breathed the fresh wind from the pine boughs.

Joy moved her crutches a few steps closer to the strange animal and said soothingly, "You're very pretty. Won't you come down to me?"

The sound of her voice and the sigh of the wind made the little animal tremble with fear. Noticing its fear,

Joy spoke more softly.

"Don't be afraid of me," she said. "I won't hurt you."

Joy's blond ponytail had a blue ribbon tied around it. She wore a blue and white print dress with small blue bows on the short sleeves.

"Please come down to me," she coaxed. "I can't climb up there to you, so you come down here to me! We can play together!"

If the animal understood what she was saying, it didn't respond. It stood near the tree, trembling like the pine needles on the green boughs above it.

"I wonder what your name is," Joy continued. "Daddy would call you 'Snowball.' He sometimes calls me 'Joyful' to tease me, but my real name is Joy."

When she said "Snowball," she thought the animal understood, for it turned its head and looked directly at her.

"'Snowball'," she said again. "You're Snowball, and I'm Joy. Won't you come down here to me? You have pink eyes, don't you? If I could only come closer..."

The animal did not move. It stood as if it were rooted in the rocky soil like one of the old trees.

"Well, if you won't come down here, I'm going to try to climb up there," Joy declared.

She started up the steep slope on her crutches. It was hard for her to swing her body uphill, moving one crutch at a time. After she had struggled a few steps, she

looked up to see the animal trying to move. It was lame, too. It could not use the leg it had been resting.

"You're hurt!" Joy exclaimed softly. "I won't take another step toward you. I don't want to hurt you. Is your leg broken, Snowball?"

The frightened animal tried to walk again, but this time it fell down.

"You poor thing!" Joy said. "I'm going home to get Daddy. I have to leave now, but I'll be back very soon."

She turned on her crutches, taking a step at a time. Hopping nimbly like a wild rabbit, she swung herself down to the path and hurried toward home.

Joy's mother was crumbling cornbread onto the ground for her chickens when she heard Joy approaching. She was startled to see her daughter hurrying recklessly up the path from the woods.

"Mama, where's Daddy?" Joy shouted excitedly.

"What's the matter with you?" her mother asked. "You're almost out of breath! You know you shouldn't run! You might fall…"

"I don't have time for that now, Mama!" Joy interrupted. "I've found the prettiest little animal I've ever seen! It's got ears that stand out like a calf's and long slender legs! It's white, and it's got pink eyes!"

"Pink eyes!" her mother repeated. "You never saw an animal like that, Joy Burton! It's your imagination

14

again! Remember, you once told us you saw a squirrel with pink toenails!"

"Now if you want your father, he's out at the barn. If you want him to listen to you, don't tell him the animal you've found has pink eyes!"

Helen Burton nervously watched her daughter start across the yard toward the barn. "Don't be so reckless, Joy!" she warned.

Joy was much too excited to follow her mother's advice. She hobbled to the fence, opened the gate, and hurried across the barnlot to her father, who was planting sweet corn in freshly plowed furrows.

"Daddy, Daddy, I've found something!" she shouted.

"What have you found, Joyful?" her father asked.

"A white animal with slender legs and ears like a calf's," she replied. "And it has pretty pink eyes, Daddy!"

"Now come, come, Joy," he chided her. "It can't have pink eyes!"

"Honest it has, Daddy!" she sighed breathlessly. "I got close enough to see its eyes!"

"Is it tame?" her father asked.

"No, it's not tame," Joy replied. "It trembled and was afraid of the sound of the wind. It was afraid of me, too!"

"But Joy, how did you get close enough to see that its eyes are pink?"

Joy was silent for a moment, then she said very

seriously, "It can't walk, Daddy. It's lame, too."

Don Burton turned his head so she wouldn't see the tears that welled up in his eyes. He felt very deeply for his only daughter, who had been crippled by polio. Her left leg was lame.

"I'm sure you've found something, Joyful," he said kindly. "But I don't know any animal but a mink or a weasel that has pink eyes! And they're very small. You say this one is as large as a spindle-legged calf?"

"Yes, he is," she said. "Come with me and I'll show you!"

Joy's father set his basket of seed corn on the ground and said, "All right, I'll go with you! Let's go see what you've found!"

Joy hopped across the barnlot ahead of her father.

"Come along, Helen!" Don called. "Let's go see what Joy's found! She says she's found an animal that looks like a white calf with pink eyes!"

"Yes, that's what she told me," Helen replied. "Remember the squirrel with painted toenails?"

"She's beyond that imaginary stage now," Don said. "Let's go see what she's found."

Joy was soon far ahead of her parents. She was hopping as fast as her crutches would permit.

"Come on!" she called back. "It's down by the cliffs! Follow the path!"

"There's no point in telling her to slow down, Don,"

Helen said. "She's too excited to listen."

Joy hurried down the path toward the cliffs, and was soon around a bend and out of sight. Don and Helen followed.

When her parents caught up to her, Joy had stopped near the cliffs. She pointed up the slope and cried, "Look up there!"

"It looks like a white deer!" her father said. "This is hard to believe!"

"It does have pink eyes, Don!" Helen said.

Helen Burton was a tall, slender woman, and very pretty. Her eyes were as blue as her daughter's, and her hair was honey-colored.

"Yes, it's a white deer!" Don said. "It must be an albino. This is the first time I ever saw an albino deer, but I've read about them. I wonder where it came from? There aren't any deer in this county."

"It may have come from the McKinley Game Reserve across the Ohio River," Helen suggested.

"But, Mama, it would have had to swim the river!" Joy said. "And the Game Reserve is fifty miles away!"

"Deer can swim," her father reminded her, "and they can travel fast. A deer can travel that far in a day. Maybe this fawn swam the river with its mother because of a food shortage on the reserve."

"Dogs may have killed the mother and missed getting this little one," Helen added.

"Then it is up to us to take care of little Snowball," Joy said.

"Snowball! That's the right name for this deer," her father said. "You picked a good one."

"I knew that's what you would've named this little animal, Daddy, so I named it for you," Joy said proudly.

"Don, is it a male or a female?" Helen asked.

"I don't know, but we'll soon see," Don said, as he started climbing the steep slope. "But whether it's a male or female, it will be named Snowball just the same!"

When the little deer saw Joy's father climbing toward it, it acted as if it wanted to run. It stood trembling for a moment, then took three steps and toppled over.

"It's a male fawn," Don called softly, as he sat down beside the shaking animal. "It's scared to death. You know, Joy," he called, "a male deer is called a buck. You could call him 'Buck'. That would be a good name, too."

"But I like Snowball better! Don't you, Mama?"

"Yes, I do," her mother agreed.

"Bring him down, Daddy, so we can see him," Joy called.

Don Burton picked up the young deer and came down the steep slope to the path, where Joy and her mother waited.

"Oh, Daddy, how pretty he is!" Joy exclaimed.

"He's a beautiful animal, all right," her father said.

Speaking slowly and seriously, he added, "But we might not be able to save him. If he hadn't been hurt badly, he would have run away from us."

"What's wrong with him, Don?" Helen asked.

"When I put my hand on his left hip, I thought I could feel the bone move," he replied. "The hip must be broken."

"What will we do if it is broken, Daddy?" Joy asked.

"I don't know," Don sighed. "We can't do much, I'm afraid."

"We'll have to do something!" Joy declared.

"Please take him in the house," Joy said to her father when they got back home with the fawn.

"You know we never allow animals inside!" her mother said quickly.

"But Snowball's so afraid and so helpless, Mama! He needs our help!" Joy pleaded.

"I agree with her," Don said. Still holding the trembling fawn in his arms, he sat down on the edge of the porch. "I've held many kinds of wild animals in my arms before, but none of them were as afraid as Snowball is now!"

"How old do you think he is?" Helen asked.

"I don't think he can be over three weeks old," Don answered.

Joy smoothed the rumpled hair on Snowball's back

and spoke soothingly to him. She had grown up talking to wild animals and birds. She had fed and talked to them until they had accepted her.

"I'm almost sure Snowball's hip is broken, Joy," said her father. "I can feel the break, and when I touch his hip, he flinches. That's too bad."

"What do you mean?" Joy asked quickly.

"He might have to be put out of his misery," Don said. "I'm sorry."

"What do you mean, Daddy?" Joy repeated haltingly.

"I mean I might have to put him to sleep," he told her.

"You can't, Daddy!" Joy protested. "Because he has a broken leg, you mean he has to die? You had a doctor for my leg! Can't you get one for Snowball?"

Helen Burton looked at her daughter, who was trying unsuccessfully not to cry. "Let's do something, Don," she pleaded.

Joy sat down beside her father and leaned her crutches against the porch.

"You poor thing," she wept. "You're lost, and you have no mother and father. You were just talking, weren't you, Daddy? You couldn't kill him, could you?"

"No, Joy, I couldn't," Don admitted.

Joy's plea for the deer's life had aroused the tenderness in her father. If there had ever been the instinct of the hunter in him, it was gone now.

"Let's take Snowball in the house, Daddy," Joy said happily. "He can lie on my bed while you go and get the animal doctor."

Don looked at Helen to see if she approved of his taking Snowball inside. She nodded.

Joy followed her father into the house. He carried the fawn into her room and gently laid him on the bed.

"He won't jump off, will he?" Joy asked nervously.

"No, he's not able to," her father replied.

Joy sat down on the edge of the bed and began stroking Snowball's face. The deer was still in pain, but he no longer trembled. He seemed to sense that he was among friends.

"There are two vets in Auckland, Helen," Don said. "Which one should I get?"

"Dr. Martin," his wife answered quickly. "He saved Wampler's dog after a car ran over her and broke three legs. The Wamplers thought she'd never walk again, but she's fine now."

"Then he ought to be able to save Snowball—he only has one broken leg," Joy added cheerfully.

"I'll get Dr. Martin," Don said. "I'll be back as soon as I can."

He stopped on his way out the door and turned to look at Joy. She was still stroking the deer's face and talking to him. She seemed very sure that he was going to live and be her friend.

Joy sat beside Snowball and spoke comfortingly to him while she waited for her father to return. She told him Dr. Martin would soon come and relieve him of his pain. She told him how doctors could set broken bones and make them grow strong again. Snowball didn't seem to understand what she was saying, but the sound of her voice soothed him.

The ground hog whose home was up among the cliffs hadn't understood her at first, but later he had come to understand her quite well. He even learned to stand on his hind feet and whistle for a cracker, so she called him "Old Cracker."

The birds understood her, too. They had become tame enough to alight on her and to eat from her hands. Joy was sure that Snowball would soon learn to trust her as her other animal friends did.

She never fed the little gray lizards, but she did talk to them. When she spoke to them, they would stop and listen. They turned their heads first to one side, then to the other, as if they were trying to hear what she was saying.

She once saw a lizard lying on the branch of an oak tree. Its rough, scaly skin was the same color as the bark on which it lay. When a fly flew over the lizard, it reached up and caught the unsuspecting insect in its mouth.

After about an hour had passed, Joy said, "It's about time for Dr. Martin to get here. He's going to make you well again." Snowball wiggled his ears, and she laughed merrily.

Joy's mother opened the door to see if someone was in the room with her. She knew Joy talked to animals, birds, and dolls, but never before had she heard so much talking and laughing. Helen listened a few minutes, then quietly closed the door. She had rarely seen her daughter in such a gay, talkative mood.

Soon Joy recognized the sound of her father's footsteps on the porch. She heard her mother join him, then both of them walked into her room.

"Where is Dr. Martin?" she asked.

"He'll be here soon," her father replied. "When I told him I wanted him to treat an albino deer, he was very excited. He said he'd never seen one."

"I see Dr. Martin's car pulling in now," Helen said, as she looked out the window. Don hurried out to bring him in.

Joy heard her father greet Dr. Martin at the door; then both men walked into her room. Dr. Martin was a tall man with brown eyes and black hair.

"Dr. Martin, this is my wife, Helen," Don said. "And this is our daughter, Joy."

"And this is Snowball!" Joy added.

"I'm glad to meet you, Mrs. Burton. And I'm glad to know you and Snowball, Joy. He's a very handsome patient. I've never doctored one like him before!"

The veterinarian sat down on the edge of the bed and began to examine the injured deer, as Joy watched anxiously.

"Now don't be afraid of me, Snowball," Dr. Martin said, as he put his hand on the little deer's left hip. "I've come to help you. Joy and I both want you to live."

"Yes we do, Doctor!" Joy agreed enthusiastically. "I've been telling him that you can make him well!"

"I'll certainly try to, Joy," Dr. Martin said seriously. "He's one of the most beautiful animals I've ever seen."

"What did I tell you?" Joy said to her parents. "Did you hear what Dr. Martin said?"

"Yes, we know he's pretty and that you want to keep him," her father said gently.

Dr. Martin sighed softly, and shook his head sadly. He looked at Joy's father and said, "I'm afraid you were right, Don. This deer does have a broken hip."

He stood up, then said in a low voice, "I hate to tell you this, Joy, but I can't do anything to save this fawn. I'm afraid he'll have to be put to sleep."

"No!" Joy screamed. "He will not be! I won't let him be killed!"

"Can't we save him, Dr. Martin?" Don pleaded. "Can't we save him for Joy's sake?"

"Well, there is one thing we could try," Dr. Martin said reflectively. "It would be expensive and it would take time. If we decide to try it, there would be about one chance in a hundred that this frail fawn could survive."

"Let's take that chance," Don Burton said decisively.

"Will that be necessary, Don?" Helen asked. "Joy, you may have to see Snowball die anyway, and it would be a shame for him to suffer needlessly."

"I want him to live as long as he can!" Joy sobbed.

Her mother turned and walked away from the bed. "I don't know," she sighed. "Maybe we should go by what Dr. Martin advises."

"Now I didn't say there wasn't any chance," Dr. Martin said. "I said there was about one chance in a hundred."

"I want Snowball to live," Joy said. "I don't want him to die! I want him to stay right here in my room so I can take care of him!"

"I'll make this decision right now," her father said. "Snowball's already in her room, and here's where he'll live or die."

"But this house isn't a barn," her mother protested. "We can put him in the barn if we want to take that one chance in a hundred."

"He wouldn't be safe there, Mama!" Joy said. "Dogs could get to him. I want him in here where I can take care of him!"

Dr. Martin, Helen, and Don walked out of Joy's room, and Helen closed the door behind them. Then she turned to face her husband and said, "Don, we've got a smokehouse where we can put the deer. I hate to have a sick deer in the house. Joy won't be able to take care of him. She does well to take care of herself!"

"If she wants her deer in this room," Don stated firmly, "I'll see to it that she has him there."

"Dr. Martin, you see my point of view, don't you?" Helen asked.

"Yes, Mrs. Burton, I do, but I can't make this decision. You and your husband will have to do that."

"You're right, Doctor," Don said quickly, then went on more slowly. "But I want both of you to understand how I feel. I am a strong man. I've always been strong and active—yet she—yet she—"

He halted, for he seemed unable to find the right words. He sighed, then began speaking very quietly.

"What I'm trying to say is that my daughter has been cheated like thousands of others. What promise does life hold for her? Life doesn't hold anything as hopeful for her as it did for her mother and for me in our youth! Her sympathies for Snowball are deep. And no wonder! She knows what it is to be lame!"

"I will not spare the house, money, or anything else to save that deer. I wish I could put all the polio germs in a vise and tighten it until they could never harm another child. I've had these thoughts so many times when I've seen Joy try to walk and fall!"

Helen Burton walked over to her husband and said very softly, "I didn't know you felt this way, Don. Go ahead and put the deer in her room. I guess I can handle a little extra housework."

Don Burton kissed his wife on the cheek, then left the house and went to the barn. When he returned, he was carrying a saw, a hatchet, a hammer, and other tools.

"Now, Doc," he said, "you tell me what you want, and I'll come as near as the next one to doing it for you. I'll pay you for your time. I want you to save this deer's life. I don't care what it costs or how long it takes."

"We must find a joist to tie ropes to," Dr. Martin said. "We'll have to use ropes to hold Snowball up so his hip will heal."

"Don," Helen advised, "if you need to find a joist to tie the ropes around, look for a row of nails. Start cutting on either side of the row."

"How do you know where the joists are?" Don asked.

"If you had painted this room as many times as I have, you'd know, too," Helen said.

Don stepped up in a chair. He chopped a small hole on either side of a joist. Then he put one rope over it as Dr. Martin had directed. Helen had left the room.

When Don was about through cutting the holes for the second rope, Helen came back with a tarpaulin she had found in the smokehouse. "We can put this over the floor to keep it clean," she said.

Dr. Martin spread the tarpaulin on the floor.

"Everybody's working for you now, Snowball," Joy said happily. "Be patient just a little longer!"

Helen helped make a sling for the fawn from some old sheets, and Don helped Dr. Martin attach the ropes to it.

"Now we want to arrange this so he can bear a little weight on three legs but take all the weight off his broken hip," Dr. Martin explained. "We want to give his hipbone a chance to heal."

The veterinarian put Snowball's injured leg in splints, then he and Don placed Snowball in the sling and harness they had improvised and hung from the ceiling.

"I know he must be hungry," Joy said. "What does he eat?"

"The best way to feed him is to put him on the milk of a particular cow," Dr. Martin answered. "Do you have a bottle and a nipple?"

"Yes, I think we do," Helen said.

"He'll like green things," Dr. Martin added. "Give him some clover, and cabbage leaves, too. If his health turns for the better, he'll be a great eater. If it turns for the worse, he won't eat anything. Now, can you fix a bottle for him?"

"Yes, I can do that," Helen said.

"That's a strange-looking contraption," Dr. Martin said as he looked at the harness. "It looks like a saddle with a real broad girth."

"It's a strange-looking sight, all right," Don agreed.

"It seems odd to see this in the house," Helen sighed, "but we'll get used to it."

"When will you come back, Dr. Martin?" Joy asked.

"I'll drive out tomorrow afternoon to see how Snowball is doing," the doctor replied.

"Do you hear that, Snowball?" Joy asked. "Dr. Martin will make you well so you can run and jump again!"

Dr. Martin turned to go, then stopped, and said, "I almost forgot to tell you how much milk to feed him. Give him a half-pint at first, then wait a couple of hours and give him another half-pint. If you have an alarm clock, set it for midnight and feed him again. He needs to get some strength back."

Joy looked fondly at Snowball, who was busily trying to get out of his harness. "Take it easy," she warned. "You'll have to live this way for a little while. You'll have to sleep standing up. Don't go to sleep now, though—Daddy's coming with your supper."

She looked out the window and watched her father walk across the yard. He had gone to milk the cows. She listened to the sound of his steps as he walked across the porch and came through the living room. When he came into her room, Joy could see that he was very happy.

"Snowball, Daddy has got your supper," she said. "You'd better drink your milk if you want to get well."

"You try to feed him," her father said. "You know how, don't you?"

"Yes," Joy said as she climbed out of bed. She hopped over to Snowball and said soothingly, "You've lost your mama. You must be very, very hungry!"

"That's Old Daisy's milk," her father told her. "Snowball will like it if he's not hurt too badly to eat."

"Daddy, he doesn't even try!" Joy said, as she tried unsuccessfully to put the bottle nipple into Snowball's mouth. "Maybe he doesn't know how!"

"He doesn't know what it is," her father said. "Maybe I can help you. Do you suppose I would scare him?"

"You might, Daddy. Wait a minute! I'll press milk from the bottle into his mouth so he can taste it."

Joy put her arm around the fawn's neck and held the bottle to his mouth, then forced some milk into it. At first he worked his jaws as if he were trying to yawn, then he licked out his tongue.

"He's trying now, Daddy!" Joy cried excitedly.

She was smiling now. Her ponytail, almost as white as Snowball's hair, was bobbing up and down every time she moved.

"He's catching on," her father said. "Keep on working with him. He's going to eat, I believe. If he does, that's a good sign."

"Look, Daddy, he's tasting, and he likes the taste. Look! Oh, Daddy, watch him!"

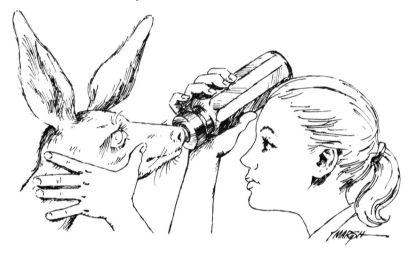

The starved fawn had learned what was in the bottle and how to get it. He sucked hungrily at the nipple to get the warm sweet milk.

"Yes, he's learning fast," her father said happily. "The poor thing must be awfully hungry. I'll bet he hasn't eaten for days! That bottle won't last long!"

"Daddy, he's so hungry!" Joy said. "Would another bottle hurt him?"

"Dr. Martin said not to give him too much," her father cautioned her. "We must follow his orders. You have to follow your doctor's orders, don't you? You can feed Snowball again at nine, and I'll feed him at midnight."

"All right," Joy said. "That's a deal!"

"I'll bring his milk at nine," Don told her. "You lie down and rest. You must be tired."

Joy took a long hop to her bed as if she were playing hopscotch in the yard.

When Joy came to the breakfast table the next morning, she said, "I dreamed of Snowball last night! I never had a more wonderful dream!"

"That's nice," her mother said, then asked, "Do you have your arithmetic assignment for today?"

"Yes," Joy replied.

"What about your grammar exercise?"

"I have that, too."

"I've fed Snowball this morning," her father told her.

"Did he eat?"

"Just like he was starved to death."

After they had eaten and Helen had finished washing the dishes, she walked into Joy's room and said, "Now we'll have your lessons. I'm an hour late—this place isn't like it once was! Not since we've added a young animal to the household!"

At one time Helen Burton had planned to be a teacher, but when she was a sophomore in Blakesburg High School, she had met Don Burton, a young farmer going from house to house selling peaches. Two years later she became Mrs. Don Burton and left Blakesburg to live on Don's farm. Now she was a teacher for only one pupil, her daughter Joy. She had given Joy most of her elementary schooling at home because Joy had been crippled by polio when she had just begun the fourth grade.

Helen pulled the small blackboard from the closet. She placed a chair in front of it so Joy could sit there and work her problems with chalk.

"Now, you watch me, Snowball!" Joy said laughingly. "You might learn arithmetic, too!"

"School has begun, Joy," her mother reminded her. Then she gave her daughter six of the most difficult problems in her textbook. Joy worked all six problems very quickly. She surprised her mother, who never knew when she found time to study.

"Now, explain each problem," her mother said.

Joy explained each correctly.

"I don't know how you do it!" her mother said.

From morning until noon her mother gave her lessons in grammar, history, science, and health, and asked her questions about them. In health, her favorite subject, Joy never missed a question. Then her mother told her to write a theme. Joy wrote a story about Old Cracker meeting Snowball down by the cliffs. When she read her theme aloud, her mother laughed.

"Mama, you're disturbing school!" Joy said. "What will Snowball think?"

"How can you write such a funny theme?" her mother asked.

"I've got more themes to write for you! I want to write about all my animal friends."

"I want your father to read this theme! I'm giving you a good grade on this one!" "You know," Mrs. Burton said, "I've never met Old Cracker! You must introduce me to him."

"I'll be glad to, Mama!"

"Do you think Old Cracker will like Snowball?"

"Oh yes!" Joy replied. "Snowball's shy and gentle. Just look at him, Mama."

"He looks like he'd run from 'most any animal, even a rabbit or a chipmunk," her mother agreed.

"That's why the other animals will like him," Joy explained. "I'll bet the birds will light on his back when I take him down to the cliffs with me."

"Do you suppose I could go down there with you someday, Joy?"

"Yes, but you'll have to be really friendly before my friends will come out for you. If you're not, the animals will hide in their dens, and the birds will fly away."

Her mother smiled pleasantly.

"That's the way you'll have to smile, Mama," Joy said approvingly.

Chapter Two

"Well, how is our little friend?" Dr. Martin asked when Joy opened the door. "Is he still alive?"

"He's not well, Dr. Martin," she replied sadly.

"He's still alive, isn't he?"

"Oh, yes, Mama and Daddy are with him now."

"I'm sorry to hear the fawn isn't doing too well," Dr. Martin said as he entered Joy's room. Joy winked at her parents so they wouldn't spoil her joke.

"I suppose he won't eat at all," Dr. Martin sighed.

"That's right, Doc," Don Burton said. "I've brought a bottle of milk to show you."

"You don't have to show me," Dr. Martin said. "When an animal is really sick, he can't eat. Don't take it too hard, Don. I know how you feel. I couldn't sleep last night for thinking about this deer and how much your daughter wants him to live."

"Look at the poor thing, Doc!" Don said as he put the bottle to Snowball's mouth. He could hardly keep from laughing. "See, he won't..."

Before he could finish, Snowball lunged for the bottle. The fawn caught the nipple in his mouth, thrust his small white head forward, and shut his pink eyes. Joy, Don, and Helen exploded with laughter. Dr. Martin was obviously stunned. He watched the fawn push forward and swish his tail with glee as he drank the warm sweet milk.

"And we thought he wouldn't live!" Dr. Martin said incredulously.

"I told you he'd live," Joy said.

Dr. Martin smiled at her and said, "You were right. You found him in time to save him."

"I brought him a basket of clover from the meadow this afternoon," Joy said. "I've never seen an animal eat the way he does."

"I fed him this afternoon, and he ate like a pig," Helen said.

"Well, I won't have to come tomorrow," Dr. Martin said. "Since Snowball is getting along so well, I'll stay away for a few days. If something happens, you let me know."

"Dr. Martin, he's so hungry all the time I wonder if we're feeding him enough," Helen said.

"How much are you feeding him?"

"A half-pint of milk six times a day and one at midnight."

"Seven half-pints," the doctor said thoughtfully. "Make it eight tomorrow. Feed him at midnight just tonight. Don't do it tomorrow. If he's still better day after tomorrow, give him an extra half-pint until he gets a quart morning, noon, and night."

Snowball nudged at Don's hand when he took the empty bottle from him. He swished his tail furiously because there wasn't any more.

"This is really a pleasant surprise for me," Dr. Martin said. "I'd better look at the splints and then be on my way."

"How long will Snowball have to be in his sling?" Joy asked.

"Until his hip heals satisfactorily. It will take three weeks, maybe longer."

Dr. Martin looked at the old sheets they had used to make the sling. He examined the rope harness that the sling was attached to, then examined the splints.

"Everything is all right here," he said. "Nothing's pressing or rubbing. These splints are tight enough. Joy, I'm as pleased as you are to save Snowball. There's only one albino in every ten thousand births! He'll be a pretty animal when he gets well."

"Do you think he'll make a good playmate, Dr. Martin?"

"The best in the world," he replied. He picked up his medicine bag, then added, "But he might jump over the fence into your Daddy's garden!"

"He'd better not," Don said. He winked at Dr. Martin. "Snowball and I won't get along when he starts that."

37

"Snowball won't have to eat your garden plants, Daddy," Joy said confidently. "He'll have a big meadow full of clover."

"But he'll like to go where you don't want him to," Dr. Martin said with a chuckle. "Never mind though—he'll never eat more than his share."

"When will you be back, Doc?" Don asked.

"In about four or five days. But if he should not get along as well as we expect him to, you let me know, and I'll be here."

Another week came and passed quickly. The Burtons followed Dr. Martin's orders, and Helen continued to conduct school for Joy five half-days of each week. This was Joy's last year of school at home. Next year she would go to the State School for the Handicapped.

Feeding Snowball was a pleasant duty for Joy. She warmed the milk for him as her father had done, and she increased the amount she fed him as Dr. Martin had prescribed. She went to the meadow and gathered baskets of clover for him, too.

When Joy went to the cliffs to see her friends, Old Cracker came trotting up to get his food.

"Cracker, don't you get jealous!" Joy scolded him. "I'll be back with all of you when Snowball gets better. I'll bring him down as soon as he gets well."

Cracker stood up on his hind legs and took crackers from her hands with his forepaws. His long, sharp toenails reminded Joy of honey-locust thorns.

Birds flew in from all directions and alighted in the trees around her. Bluebirds, cardinals, sparrows, thrushes, and catbirds came. Joy placed baby-chick feed on the tops of stumps and stones along the path.

The gray squirrels came down from the tall trees, and the striped chipmunks came from holes in the ground. They ran in front of her with their tails arched over their backs. They were always glad to see her come.

"I'll be back," she said when she had finished spreading the grain she had brought. "I have to take a basket of clover to Snowball. He's not as free as you are!"

On her way back home, she sat down in the meadow and filled her basket with clover. Bluebirds alighted in an apple tree beside the road. They sat among the white blossoms and sang songs she had heard many times before. A pair of redbirds flew over the meadow through the bright April wind. Joy looked up and saw Old Cracker trotting across the meadow.

"Where are you going, Cracker?" she called. He didn't stop, but went on toward the far side of the meadow.

"I'll bet Mrs. Cracker's got little Crackers!" Joy

exclaimed. "And you don't want me to know where they are!"

Joy picked up her basket of clover and headed down the path toward home. When she got near the house, she saw a car drive up and stop. Dr. Martin had returned to see his patient.

When Joy reached the house, Dr. Martin and her father and mother were in her room with Snowball. Dr. Martin was examining the harness that held the sling up.

"Do you want to sell Snowball to me?" he asked teasingly.

"No," Joy replied seriously. "I wouldn't part with him for anything."

"I was just teasing you, Joy," Dr. Martin said with a chuckle. Then he went on, "But I'm not teasing you when I say you're going to have a well deer one of these days. His hip is healing all right. We'll have to be careful to keep him where he is so he can't hurt himself."

Joy held the basket of clover up to Snowball's nose. He began to eat as if he were starving.

"He likes clover better than a rabbit does," Dr. Martin commented.

"When will we be able to let him down?" Joy asked.

"In about two weeks."

"That's a long time for him to have to swing there."

"While he's getting along well, we want to leave

him alone," Dr. Martin explained. "I have to go now, but I'll be back in about a week. Keep on feeding him a quart of milk at morning, noon, and night, and give him fresh clover each afternoon."

He pulled a small cigar from his inside coat pocket and lit it with his lighter. As he walked across the yard toward his car, he left a trail of light blue smoke behind him.

May came with its blue skies and mellow winds, but Snowball was still confined to Joy's room. The only time he got to breathe the fresh spring wind was when Joy's father opened the doors and windows to let the wind sweep through. Each time he cleaned the tarpaulin, he also cleaned the room with wind fresh from the meadow.

One afternoon after Joy had been to the cliffs to feed her friends and to the meadow to gather clover for Snowball, she noticed an unfamiliar car parked at the edge of the yard when she got back to the house.

She hurried inside to see who the visitor could be. She was surprised to find her own physician, Dr. Charles Vidt, talking to her parents.

Dr. Vidt was a large man with broad shoulders, blue eyes, and graying hair. Joy thought he was the kindest man she had ever known.

"Oh, Dr. Vidt," she exclaimed breathlessly, "it's so

good to see you!"

"I hear you have a surprise for me, young lady," he said affectionately.

"Then you've heard about Snowball?"

"Yes, I have," he replied, "but I haven't seen him yet."

"Come along and I'll introduce you to him," Joy said gaily. "You can watch him eat clover!"

Dr. Vidt followed Joy into her bedroom with her parents to visit the convalescing fawn. When Snowball caught sight of Joy and her basket of clover, he shook his head and swished his tail furiously.

"How beautiful he is!" Dr. Vidt exclaimed. "An albino fawn! He's the first one I've ever seen!"

"He knows me," Joy said proudly. "That's why he's switching his tail and shaking his head."

She crossed the room in three long hops. She laid one crutch on the floor, put her arm around the fawn's neck, and held out the basket of clover. The fawn ate the clover like a pet rabbit.

"Snowball, I'd like you to meet Dr. Vidt. Dr. Vidt, this is Snowball," Joy said merrily.

Dr. Vidt laughed, then bowed and said, "I'm delighted to make your acquaintance, Snowball."

Snowball, however, was more interested in his clover than he was in Dr. Vidt, whom he ignored completely.

"Who's Snowball's doctor?" Dr. Vidt asked.

"Dr. Martin," Joy replied. "Snowball's hip was broken when I found him, but Dr. Martin saved him."

"It looks as if he's done a fine job, all right," Dr. Vidt agreed.

"Snowball will soon be able to walk again," Joy said confidently. She hesitated, then asked haltingly, "Dr. Vidt, do you suppose I'll ever be able to walk without my crutches?"

"That's why I'm here today, Joy. I want to discuss that possibility with you and your parents," he replied. "I want you to be able to throw away your crutches someday soon."

"I'd like that," Joy said softly.

"Of course you would!" Dr. Vidt said, smiling affectionately at her. "Now you just listen and let me do some explaining."

"Only your left leg was affected by the polio. With proper treatment and exercise, that leg can be stimulated to seventy-five percent of normal growth. Of course, I'd have to operate to graft some muscle tissue, and your foot needs surgery, too."

"You need to operate on her foot, too?" Helen interrupted to ask.

"Yes," Dr. Vidt replied briskly. "Joy's foot has become twisted. The only way I can remedy this is to operate and transplant good muscles and tendons to

44

replace those that are not functioning. I'll do some grafting on the leg muscles, too. After the operation, I'll put a plaster cast on Joy's leg and..."

"But that means I'll have to stay in bed for weeks!" Joy complained.

"Yes, but after I take the cast off, you'll be able to walk without crutches," Dr. Vidt said.

"Could I run with Snowball? Could I go to the cliffs to see my friends?" Joy asked enthusiastically.

"The more you run and play, the better it will be for you," Dr. Vidt assured her. "Your leg and foot will need exercise. After we remove the plaster cast, they will also have to be massaged several times a day. You can do that for her, can't you, Mrs. Burton?"

"Of course! I'll do whatever I can to help," Helen replied.

"What will you do when I go to the hospital, Snowball?" Joy asked. "I want you taken care of while I'm gone!"

"I'll see to that, too," her mother promised.

"I'd like to wait until Snowball can walk again before I go," Joy said.

"You can do that," Dr. Vidt assured her. "Just let me know when you want me to make arrangements at the Toniron Hospital."

"All right, Doctor," Helen said.

"That's all I have to tell you right now, so I guess

I'd better be on my way," Dr. Vidt said as he started to the door. He stopped in the doorway, looked back at Joy, and said reflectively, "You know, I once had a little girl. She had a white ponytail, too. Unfortunately for me, she had to grow up."

Chapter Three

"Now stand still, Mr. Snowball," Dr. Martin said. "I'm not going to cut your tail off! It's too short now."

"Doc, your cigar smoke might be what's making Snowball jump like that," Don suggested.

"So Mr. Snowball doesn't like to smell strong smoke!" Dr. Martin said. "Well, well, soon he'll be smelling the fresh spring wind."

It was a clear, mild afternoon. Everyone was happy but Snowball, who didn't understand what was happening.

"Snowball, mind your manners!" Joy scolded him. "Behave yourself and let Dr. Martin take you out of that harness so you can be free again."

"I'll have freedom, too," her father said. "I've been Snowball's cleanup man for almost a month now!"

"And our home can be arranged for the family again," Helen added.

"You don't mean Snowball won't be allowed back inside, do you?" Joy protested.

"Only in an emergency," Helen said firmly.

"Mister Snowball, I want to examine you one last

time before I let you all the way down," Dr. Martin said as he inspected the hip which had been broken. He nodded approvingly, then said, "This really healed! If it ever breaks again, it will have to be in some other place."

Dr. Martin began removing the splints from Snowball's leg. He was obviously proud of his success.

"It's wonderful to have a break heal this well," he said enthusiastically. "We didn't think he had much of a chance to survive, did we, Don?"

"No, we didn't," Don replied.

"He'll have to exercise his legs to get the stiffness out," Dr. Martin explained. "He might hobble around on three legs for a few days, but he won't do that very long."

"Three legs to him are much better than one leg is to me," Joy said. "He has three-fourths of his walking power with three good legs. I have half my walking power with one good leg. He has a fourth more than I have."

"Somebody's teaching you arithmetic," Dr. Martin said.

"Mama is," Joy said proudly.

"If this deer could talk, he'd thank you, Joy," Dr. Martin told her.

"He'd thank you, too, Dr. Martin. You've saved his leg!"

"I'll get to your harness next, Snowball," Dr. Martin said. "I'll let down the ropes and get you out of the sling. It won't be long until you can go outside. We'll let Don carry you out."

Dr. Martin worked silently for several minutes, then stood up to survey his work. The harness and splints had been completely removed, but Snowball didn't seem to notice the change. He held his left hind leg up as if it were still in splints.

"You'll have to get that leg down, Snowball," Dr. Martin said, "and start walking as soon as you can."

"He still thinks he's in his harness and sling," Helen said. "Don't you think it would be better if he were taken outside?"

"You're right," Dr. Martin replied. "He'll react differently outside."

"It's my happy duty, Snowball, to take you out," Don said, grinning and stepping forward. "I brought you in, and I'll take you out."

Don picked up the fawn and carried him outside. Joy, Helen, and Dr. Martin followed him.

"Put him down now, Daddy!" Joy cried excitedly.

Don smiled warmly at her, then carefully lowered Snowball until three of his legs rested on the ground. He still refused to bear any weight on the leg which had been injured.

"What do you think of this world, Mister

Snowball?" Dr. Martin asked. "Is it too much for you? Does it look too big?"

"He'll be all right," Don said. "He'll be putting his leg down by sundown. Wait and see!"

"This is a big world, Snowball," Joy said softly. "Don't be afraid. Put your foot down."

Snowball didn't understand Joy's kind words. He seemed to wonder why everyone was gathered around him. He blinked his eyes and sniffed the fresh air.

"This world must seem very big to him," Dr. Martin said sympathetically. "He's got a lot to learn."

"Try to walk, Snowball! Take just one step," Joy urged. "Don't just stand there!"

Snowball looked at Joy, then moved one foot forward and took a bite of grass.

"Look! He understood me!" Joy exclaimed. "Hop with your hind legs! You can do it! Come on!"

Snowball leaned forward for another bite of grass. This threw him off balance and he had to hop to keep from falling.

"I told you you could hop!" Joy shouted. "You've done it! You've moved your bad leg!"

"He's like a boy who has had a stone bruise on his foot," Dr. Martin explained. "He was afraid to put his foot down, but now that he's put it down once, he'll soon be walking."

"Another hop!" Don shouted. "All he needs is

clover in front of him!"

"Look! He's getting his leg down, too," Dr. Martin said proudly.

"I'll bet Snowball would like to go to the meadow. There's a lot of clover there," Joy said. "Do you think he could walk that far, Dr. Martin?"

"Why don't you ask him?"

Joy laughed, then turned to Snowball and asked, "Would you like to go to the meadow with me?"

Snowball looked up at her and blinked.

"I thought so!" Joy said merrily. "Come on! I know you can do it!"

Snowball stared at Joy, who was smiling at him and beckoning to him with her hand. He stood very still, then suddenly took two long hops toward her.

"He knows she's his friend," Dr. Martin said. "Nothing could be better for him now. All that deer needs is exercise. He's going to be all right."

"I'm ready to pay you now, Dr. Martin," Don said.

"Oh, let's wait and see how Snowball gets along. I wouldn't know how to charge for this anyway—I've never doctored a deer before."

Dr. Martin turned to watch Joy, who was slowly coaxing Snowball toward the meadow. Her white ponytail was bobbing up and down on the lazy afternoon wind.

"Your daughter's love for that deer...," he sighed.

"He'll make a nice playmate for her. That's a pretty sight out there."

∞

Snowball stopped to smell the water in Shacklerun Creek. He had found clover in abundance, and now he had found cool water under the shade of a willow tree.

"Snowball, we have to go to the barn to see if Gypsy will adopt you," Joy said. "If she lets you be her calf, we won't have to fix a bottle for you. When you see Gypsy, don't be afraid."

Joy hopped along the path toward the barn, and Snowball followed close behind her. Before they reached the barn, Don and Helen joined them.

"We've got a surprise for you, Joy," Don announced.

"Do you hear that, Snowball? Daddy and Mama have a surprise for us!"

"Are you taking Snowball to see Gypsy?" Helen asked.

"Yes, Mama."

"Be careful—Gypsy might not accept him," Helen warned.

"Why not, Mama?"

"Because they're different kinds of animals."

"Your mother's right, Joy," Don said.

"We've fixed a bed of straw in the smokehouse for Snowball," Helen said. "That's our surprise!"

"That building is a strong one," Don said. "We can

put him in for the night and lock the door behind him. He'll be safe there."

Joy said, "Oh, I'm so glad! Thank you!"

When Joy, her parents, and Snowball got close to the barnlot, Gypsy put her head over the fence and looked suspiciously at the white deer. She became even more nervous when Don opened the gate and walked into the barnlot with Snowball. Gypsy thrust her head forward and stared at the white fawn. She shook her head threateningly, and Snowball trembled with fear.

"Gypsy's not friendly with Snowball," Joy sighed.

"She's not going to adopt him," Helen said. "She knows he's not her kind."

Suddenly Gypsy snorted loudly and lunged at Snowball. He was so frightened he forgot that he had ever had a broken hip. He pivoted on his hind legs and leaped up and over the fence.

"I can't believe it!" Don gasped.

"Gypsy's a mean cow!" Joy cried angrily. "Look at Snowball! He's still running!"

"But he won't run away," Don assured her. "See—he's going back to the house."

Snowball ran up to the porch and stopped. Joy hurried over to him and began stroking his face.

"Gypsy was mean to you," she whispered soothingly. "If I had known she was going to act like that, I wouldn't have taken you over there."

She turned to her father and asked, "Daddy, do you have a light in the smokehouse?"

"Yes, Joy," he replied. "Everything is ready for Snowball. I hope he'll like his new home."

The next morning, Joy dressed and ate breakfast hurriedly. She was planning to take Snowball to the cliffs to visit her other animal friends.

The grass was still wet with dew when she and Snowball started down the path that led to the cliffs. Joy carried a basket of food for the birds and animals. Snowball ambled along beside her, and she spoke to him as if he were a human companion.

"Now, Snowball, I'm taking you back where I found you," she told him. "I don't think you'll remember the place."

Soon they had reached the apple tree in which a pair of bluebirds had a nest. The male bluebird was singing a song which Joy had heard many times before.

"Is that all you've got to do, Mr. Bluebird?" she asked. "Listen, Snowball! He's singing to his mate. She's sitting on the nest now, waiting for her eggs to hatch."

Joy increased her speed as she hopped down the winding path that led out of the meadow. This path wound among moss-covered rocks and big trees.

"Snowball, our friends are everywhere," she said. "We can't see them, but they're watching us. Now, you mustn't be jealous! You must use your best manners. I want them to like you."

Joy hopped over to a large rock that was covered with gray-green lichen.

"This is a table," she explained. "It's for the birds and the squirrels. When I put their food on this table, they'll come running and flying from all directions. Don't you get scared! They won't hurt you!"

Snowball, however, was much too busy exploring to listen to what Joy was saying. He picked his way among the large stones which were scattered about on the slope below the rock cliff and sniffed at the bark of a giant pine tree.

"This is where I found you, Snowball," Joy said as she took a handful of baby-chick feed from her basket and scattered it over the lichen-covered rock. "You were afraid of everything then. Things are different now, aren't they? You don't even remember what happened to you."

"There!" she said. "That's about enough on this table."

Chipmunks came running from all directions. Snowball looked curiously at the small creatures as they came scurrying toward him.

"Look at them, Snowball!" Joy exclaimed. "They're not afraid of you! They can tell you won't hurt them."

One by one, the chipmunks jumped up onto the flat rock and began eating ravenously. Snowball walked down to the rock and slowly thrust his head forward. He tried to rub noses with a chipmunk that was sitting on its haunches and busily stuffing grain into its mouth. The chipmunk chattered excitedly and hurried to the other side of the rock. Snowball stepped back and wiggled his ears. He seemed very puzzled.

"You mustn't try to rub noses with them, Snowball! You're too big for that!" Joy said laughingly.

A pair of redbirds were perched on a branch high above Joy's head. The male redbird, whose plumage was as red as October sumac leaves, began to sing.

"Look up there in the trees, Snowball," Joy whispered. "The redbirds are waiting to see if I put food on their table. If I don't, they'll fly down and eat with the chipmunks."

Joy picked up her basket and hopped over to a tree stump, with Snowball following close behind her.

"When they cut down this tree, they made a perfect table for my birds," Joy said, as she spread grain over the flat, smooth top of the stump.

The male redbird flew down and circled the table once. When he saw that there was no danger, he alighted on the top of the stump and called to his mate. She flew down to him and both began to eat the grain.

"More birds will come soon, Snowball," Joy whispered. "Look! There's another redbird!"

The three redbirds were soon joined by a pair of

sparrows from Don Burton's barn. Next, several robins flew in, alighted on the stump, and began to eat, too. Soon many different kinds of birds were perched on the stump or in the trees above it.

Joy was delighted to see all her friends getting along so well together. She turned to Snowball and said happily, "The birds aren't afraid of you, either. They know you won't hurt them."

Just as Joy finished speaking, a robin flew down and alighted on her shoulder. While Snowball watched curiously, a sparrow also came down and alighted on Joy's head. The white fawn wiggled his ears and shook his head. He couldn't understand what was taking place in the enchanted world to which Joy had brought him. Suddenly, his eyes widened and he trembled with fear. A redbird had alighted on his back! Joy hurried over to him and laid her hand on his head.

"It's all right," she said. "It's only a redbird. He won't hurt you. You mustn't be afraid."

With Joy standing beside him, Snowball stopped trembling and the look of fear faded from his eyes. Joy smiled at his awkward attempts to catch a glimpse of the bird perched on his back.

When she was sure that Snowball was no longer afraid, Joy hopped over to the chipmunks' stone table and spread more grain on it. She looked up in time to see three gray squirrels hurrying down the slope.

"You're always late!" she said, pretending to scold them. "But I've got something for you, too!"

She placed handfuls of grain on the gnarled roots of an ancient beech. The squirrels came hurrying up to her and began chattering merrily when they found their food. Each sat on its haunches with its bushy tail arched over its back while it ate.

"You haven't seen everything yet, Snowball!" Joy said.

A gray lizard ran up the smooth bark of a beech tree and stopped long enough to catch a green fly.

"I don't feed the lizards. They live on insects and have to feed themselves, like the swallows that build their mud nests under the roofs of the overhanging cliffs that Daddy calls rock houses," Joy explained. She spoke to Snowball as if he could understand every word she was saying.

"Now look who's in my way, won't you?" she said to an old terrapin that was crawling slowly across the path. "I don't feed him, either," she told Snowball. "He lives on vegetables and plants in the spring and summer. In the fall when the plants die, he finds a place to hide and sleeps there until spring."

Snowball was following Joy down the path. He stopped and put his nose down close enough to touch the terrapin. When the terrapin looked up and saw the white fawn standing over him, he withdrew into his shell and closed up his black-checked armor.

"Our friends will follow us," Joy said as she scattered more chick feed on rocks and stumps. "They know where I'll leave food for them."

Suddenly a shrill whistle pierced the air. Snowball, startled by the unexpected sound, jumped. Joy looked around quickly, then began to laugh.

"Oh, it's you!" she said, when she saw Old Cracker hurrying clumsily toward her.

Seeing Old Cracker always made her laugh. He was almost as broad across his back and shoulders as he was long, and he had a short, flat tail that resembled a butter paddle. He stood upright on his short, stubby hind legs and peered first at Joy, then at the white deer beside her. Then he whistled again.

Snowball shook his head. He looked curiously at the short, pudgy ground hog. The two animals stared at one another until Old Cracker grew bored and whistled demandingly for the food Joy had brought him.

Joy took a packet of crackers from her basket. When Old Cracker saw the little package wrapped in wax paper, he began to dance around excitedly, for he knew what was inside. Joy had brought packages of crackers to him many times before. His belly, bare of the coarse gray wool that hid the rest of his body, protruded enormously. Joy looked at his naked stomach and laughed. She had just figured out why he didn't have fur on this part of his body. He had become so fat that his belly rubbed the ground.

"Don't you try to rub noses with Old Cracker," Joy warned Snowball. "He might bite you. Wait until I give him a cracker—then maybe he'll be too happy to bite you."

She tore the paper open and handed a cracker to the ground hog. He accepted it, using his forepaws as if they were hands, and sliced the cracker neatly with his long, razor-sharp front teeth. He ate it quickly and whistled for another as soon as he had finished.

"Another cracker so soon?" Joy exclaimed.

Cracker took a short step toward her and whistled again. He licked his mouth and looked eagerly up at her. He had no fear of her. He had become the most affectionate of all her small animal friends.

"Don't be so anxious," Joy said, as she tossed him another cracker.

He accepted the delicacy politely and ate it gracefully.

"See how nice he is, Snowball! He has good manners. But don't you get too close—he still might bite you!"

She took another cracker from the package.

"I wonder if you'd eat a cracker," she said, offering one to Snowball.

Snowball smelled the cracker, then gently took it

from her hand. He tasted it cautiously at first, then began crunching it rapidly. He liked the salty taste.

"Oh, you like them too, Snowball!" Joy said as she handed another to Old Cracker. "Now I've got to feed crackers to two of you! Mama will fuss about my taking so many!"

Then Joy heard a rustling in the wild gooseberry bushes near the edge of the cliff. She looked up and saw something she had never seen before. A little ground hog came from under the gooseberry bushes and ran over to Old Cracker.

"You pretty thing!" Joy exclaimed. "I'd like to pick you up and hold you in my hands!"

But she didn't attempt to catch the young ground hog. She knew that most wild animals had to be shown love and friendship for quite a long time before they would submit to being fondled.

Soon three more young ground hogs came out from beneath the gooseberry bushes and ran toward Old Cracker. Joy looked about for Mrs. Cracker, who undoubtedly was the shy member of the family. She saw her standing stone-still behind a small bush near the edge of the cliff.

"There's Mrs. Cracker, Snowball," she whispered. "Look at her! She must be very proud of her family."

She tried to give crackers to the young ground hogs, but they were afraid of her. They backed off into the bushes and disappeared.

"Cracker, I'm going to leave you some crackers and maybe you can tell your wife and children how good they are! They're afraid of me, but after they learn no one here will harm them, they'll become a part of our family."

Joy put down several crackers for the family of ground hogs. When she saw Snowball looking hungrily at them, she realized that he thought they were for him.

"Don't eat those, you greedy deer! They're for the ground hogs!" she said, as she reached into her basket. "Here—I saved a few for you."

Joy handed Snowball a cracker, then distributed the rest of the food in her basket. She spread more grain on the rocks and gnarled beech roots. When she had emptied her basket, she looked about and smiled contentedly. All her friends were happy. The birds were singing and the chipmunks and squirrels were chattering merrily. She turned to Snowball and stroked his face lovingly. Together, they started up the narrow path toward home.

Chapter Four

"I don't mind buying extra crackers," Joy's father said as he patted her cheek. "I'm glad Snowball likes crackers."

Joy was sitting on the edge of her bed. She was wearing her blue Sunday dress, and her ponytail was tied with a blue velvet ribbon. She would be leaving soon to go to the hospital in Toniron.

"Snowball likes crackers as much as Old Cracker does," she said happily. "Old Cracker's wife and their four little crackers might start coming to the cliffs to be fed, too. If they do, you'll have to buy even more crackers. You'll need a lot, Daddy, to feed the Cracker family and Snowball."

"I don't mind," Don said. "I'll see that Snowball gets crackers. I'll feed crackers to the ground hogs, too, if they're not afraid of me."

"When you get to know my friends at the cliffs, you'll love them," Joy said softly. "You'll have to go easy with them at first. You won't get to know them as soon as you think."

Helen Burton was packing a suitcase for Joy. She

included a half-dozen of her favorite dolls and some photographs of Snowball. She thought Joy might like to show these pictures to the doctors and nurses at the hospital.

"Well, I have everything ready," Helen said. "I can't think of anything I've forgotten."

"I'd like to see Snowball before I go," Joy said, as she reached for her crutches. She smiled thoughtfully and added, "I'll be throwing these crutches away one day soon."

Joy hurried out of the house and hopped across the yard to the smokehouse. She leaned her crutches against the wall and opened the door. As she hopped inside, the fawn ran up to her. "Snowball, I'll be gone for a few days," she told him. "You be good and mind your manners. I'll soon be back."

Snowball didn't understand what she was saying. He shook his head and wiggled his ears. Joy knew what he wanted.

"You can't be hungry," she scolded gently. "You've had milk and crackers. Now, stop begging!

"You're through with your hospital days, Snowball. Your hip has healed and you can run and play. Now it's my turn to go to the hospital. Dr. Vidt is going to straighten my foot so I'll be able to run and play with you. That's why I have to leave you for a while. Nothing will bother you here. You'll have plenty of milk, clover, and water—and crackers for your dessert!"

She patted the fawn's nose affectionately and laughed. Snowball jumped, kicked up his heels, and shook his head as if he were laughing, too.

"When I get back, we'll have a wonderful time together," Joy said happily.

Snowball shook his head and jumped again.

"Good-bye, Snowball," Joy said. She put her arms around his neck and hugged him. "I'll see you later. Mind your manners and be a good deer! Do what Mama and Daddy tell you."

Joy hopped out of the smokehouse and closed the door behind her. She hurried across the yard to the pickup truck. Her parents, who had waited patiently for her to say good-bye to Snowball, helped her climb into the truck.

They followed a narrow, winding road for several miles, then turned onto a busy highway that led up the broad Ohio River valley. The highway led past a wall of cliffs on the right, and there was a railroad on the left, between the highway and the river.

They soon reached a high bridge that spanned the Ohio River. Here, Joy saw something she had never seen before, the early morning sun transforming the river into a broad, wind-rippled ribbon of light. Until this time, her appointments with Dr. Vidt had always been later in the day, after the sun had climbed higher and the bright morning light had faded from the river.

They crossed the bridge and drove into the outskirts of Toniron. In a few minutes Don drove into a parking lot behind a large brick building.

"This is the hospital," he said.

Don opened the door and stepped out. Joy started to slide under the steering wheel behind him to follow.

"Just a minute, Joy," he said. "Let me tell them you're here. Sometimes the hospital is so full only the emergency patients are admitted."

He walked up the broad street to the hospital entrance. Joy and her mother settled down to wait for him to return. Joy was smiling happily. She was thinking about playing with Snowball. She could see herself running over the meadow with him. She could see herself dressed in long socks and brown loafers. She wouldn't have to go away to school, now. She wouldn't have to leave Snowball and her other animal friends.

From the truck window she watched a bird fly over the housetops and busy streets. It was carrying something in its beak. Joy watched the small, dingy-colored bird fly up to the nest it was building high on the hospital wall. She was watching the bird so intently that she forgot to watch for her father. When she finally looked away from the bird's nest, she was surprised to see her father and a hospital orderly coming toward her. The orderly was pushing a wheelchair and talking to her father.

"They're coming, Mama!" Joy exclaimed, as she scrambled across the seat. She climbed out of the truck and took three long hops without her crutches.

"Where are you going, Joy?" her father asked.

"You don't have to walk!" the orderly told her. "I've come to take you in."

Joy held onto the truck to steady herself until her father arrived and helped her hop over to the wheelchair. When she was seated comfortably, the orderly began pushing her toward the hospital entrance. Her parents walked along beside her.

"Did you see Dr. Vidt, Daddy?"

"Just for a minute," her father replied. "He was in a hurry."

"He's not going to send me home to come back another time, is he?"

"No, he'll operate at ten o'clock tomorrow morning."

"Why do I have to wait so long?" Joy asked disappointedly.

"There are several things he has to do before the operation," her father replied.

"You're the first one I've ever taken in who wasn't scared to death," the orderly said as he wheeled the chair into a large elevator.

"Room 25 will be your home for a few days," her

father told her when they arrived on the second floor.

"How many days?" Joy asked.

"Five or six, maybe seven."

"Then I'll only be away from Snowball for a week!" Joy said happily.

" Who's Snowball?" the orderly asked.

"He's a pet deer," Don replied.

"A pet deer!" the orderly exclaimed. He looked at Joy and said, "You've got a pet deer? I'll bet he'll miss you!"

"Yes, he'll miss me, but not any more than I'll miss him," Joy replied sadly.

The orderly wheeled her into Room 25, where a nurse was waiting.

"I'm Elsie O'Leary," said the nurse.

"I'm Joy Burton," Joy responded.

"Yes, we have your name down," said Miss O'Leary as she helped her out of the wheelchair. "Now, I'll excuse you gentlemen. Joy has to get undressed."

The orderly pushed the wheelchair out into the corridor, then turned to Don and said, "You've got a mighty nice daughter. I sure hope everything turns out all right for her."

When Don returned to Joy's room, he found her sitting up in her bed. Her hair had been combed and brushed, and she was wearing a white hospital gown.

"Daddy, I like this," she said. "It's a lot like my room at home. Look around!"

Miss O'Leary had set Joy's dolls on a bureau in the corner of the small room, and placed her schoolbooks, paper, and pencils on the small table beside her bed. She had also carefully arranged the photographs of Snowball on the bureau so that Joy could see them from her bed. She had placed one picture on the small table, too.

"This is nice," Don said to Miss O'Leary.

"Daddy, when are you going home?" Joy asked.

"Very soon," Don replied.

"But I'm going to stay with you tonight, Joy," her mother said reassuringly.

"But you don't have to, Mama," Joy protested. "I'm not afraid."

Just then the door opened and Dr. Vidt walked in. He was wearing a gray tweed sport coat and gray trousers.

"Good morning, sweetheart," he said jovially. "How are you feeling today?"

"I'm not sick, Dr. Vidt," Joy said. "You know what my trouble is. I'll be fine as soon as I can walk on two legs as well as Snowball can walk on four."

"Yes, I met Snowball out at your house, didn't I? How is he?"

"He was fine when I left," Joy said. "He's walking

71

as well as he ever did now. Dr. Martin made his lame leg as good as new. He even jumped over the barnlot fence!"

"What? You mean he's jumping fences now?" Dr. Vidt asked. "When I was there, you had him in a sling held up with ropes and his leg was in splints!"

"You can see he's not tied up now, Dr. Vidt," Joy said as she pointed to the picture of Snowball on her table.

"He's an unusual pet," Dr. Vidt said. "An albino deer is very rare. You're very lucky to have one for a pet."

"I'll miss Snowball while I'm here," Joy said softly.

"Who's taking care of him now?" Dr. Vidt asked.

"I am, Dr. Vidt," Don replied.

"I'm glad to hear that Snowball's getting along so well," Dr. Vidt said.

"Do you think I'll be able to run and play with Snowball soon?" Joy asked hopefully.

"I certainly hope so, Joy," her doctor said seriously. He turned to her parents and added, "I'd like to get seventy-five percent normal development back in that leg."

"Will that much let me run and play with Snowball?" Joy asked.

"It certainly will!"

"Won't that be great?" Joy exclaimed. She had no fear of being in the hospital. She was radiantly happy and there was a new look in her eyes.

Dr. Vidt smiled at Joy, then turned to Nurse O'Leary and said briskly, "I've ordered x-rays, Elsie, and you'll want to make all the necessary preparations for tomorrow morning. I'll go see my other patients, then I'll come back."

"All right, Doctor."

Dr. Vidt paused in the doorway and winked at Joy, then went hurrying off down the corridor.

"I'd better be going back now, Joyful," her father said.

"Be sure to feed Snowball!" Joy reminded him.

"I won't forget," he assured her.

"I know who Snowball is—I've seen your pictures of him," Nurse O'Leary said, "but who are all these other animals?" She took a photograph of Snowball and several other animals from the bureau and handed it to Joy.

"Those are my friends down at the cliffs. Those birds fly down from the trees and light on my shoulders and on my head."

"Are you sure they're that tame?" Miss O'Leary asked sceptically.

"Yes, they really are," Joy said quickly. "They know I won't harm them. They know I love them."

"Now if you want to get word to me between now and in the morning, you call Roy Millmore in Blakesburg and he can come to the farm in his taxi," Don said to Helen. He turned to Joy and said softly, "I must be on my way now, but I'll be back early tomorrow morning."

"I'm already dressed and waiting," Joy said the next morning when her father walked into the room. "It's going to happen soon now. I'm glad you're back."

"I had to drive fast to get here," Don said.

"Tell me about Snowball, Daddy. Was he hungry?"

"He drank his milk and ate all the crackers I gave him."

"Did you give him clover?"

"I let him get his own clover in the meadow. As soon as he got all he wanted, he ran faster than the wind toward the house and..."

"Someday soon I'll be able to run with him," Joy interrupted.

"He chased the chickens, Joy," her father went on. "He ran after them, jumping and shaking his head and pawing at the wind with his feet!"

Joy laughed until she couldn't talk.

"You've got some pet!" Nurse O'Leary exclaimed. "I didn't know a deer would chase chickens!"

"I didn't think anything would run from Snowball," Joy said. "I'm glad he's found something he can chase! Everything frightens him. If an old hen turns around and ruffles her feathers at him, he'll run the other way!"

"I didn't have any trouble getting him back in the smokehouse," her father said. "I thought I might."

"Now tell me about Old Cracker and all my other friends, Daddy."

"Your animal friends must not trust me yet," Don sighed. "I followed your instructions. I filled your basket with chicken feed, bread, and crackers. I walked down the path to the cliffs and put the feed where you told me to, but I didn't see a single animal. But I did see a few birds, and some of them flew very close to me." He smiled. "A couple of them even lit on my shoulders!"

Joy looked very surprised.

"Daddy, you don't visit my friends very often, so the animals don't know you. When they get to know you better, they'll be more friendly. But I'm surprised that the birds came to you."

Don Burton smiled again, as if he had a secret.

"Miss O'Leary, how much longer will it be before Joy goes to the operating room?" Helen asked anxiously.

The nurse looked at her wrist watch and replied, "Just a few minutes."

"Daddy, did you tell Snowball I was all right?" Joy asked.

"When I got home yesterday, I tried to talk to him the way you always do," her father replied. "I told him you were in the hospital and..."

Just then a strange nurse opened the door and

wheeled a gurney into the room.

"This is Miss Gifford. She's come to take you to the operating room," Nurse O'Leary explained.

Miss O'Leary and Miss Gifford lifted Joy onto the gurney. She was very happy and excited.

"Now, don't you worry, Mama!" she said. "Everything will be all right! Daddy, don't forget to feed Snowball."

"I won't, Joy," he promised.

"Snowball is Joy's pet deer," Nurse O'Leary told Miss Gifford. "She's told me about him. He's an albino and he has pink eyes. He had a broken hip when she found him in the woods, but he's all right now."

"How wonderful!" Miss Gifford exclaimed.

"Where's Dr. Vidt?" Joy asked.

"He's waiting for you," Miss O'Leary replied, as the two nurses wheeled her into the hall. She turned to Don and Helen, who had followed, and said softly, "I'm sorry, but this is as far as you can go with us. You can go back to Joy's room and wait if you like, or you might want to go to the coffee shop. It may be three or four hours before we bring her back to her room."

The two nurses wheeled Joy down the hall and into the elevator. As the elevator doors closed, she smiled and waved merrily to her parents, who were watching and trying very hard to look as happy as their daughter.

∞

At two o'clock that afternoon, Miss O'Leary and Miss Gifford brought Joy back to her room. She was asleep, and the nurses gently lifted her from the gurney and placed her in her bed. Then Nurse Gifford left the room with the gurney. Nurse O'Leary stayed behind to talk to the Burtons.

"Is she all right?" Helen asked anxiously.

"Yes, she's quite all right, Mrs. Burton," Miss O'Leary replied. "She's resting now, but she'll wake up soon."

"Did Dr. Vidt think the operation was successful?" Don asked.

"Yes, Mr. Burton. He wouldn't have operated if he hadn't been sure the operation would be a success," Nurse O'Leary assured him.

"When will he be in to see her?" Helen asked.

"In about thirty minutes, when she's completely awake. She's in no danger now," Miss O'Leary said. "You needn't be worried."

"I'll wait to see Dr. Vidt a few minutes before I go home to take care of the farm," Don said. "I want to be sure Joy's going to be all right." He laughed, then added, "Besides, I promised Joy I'd tell Snowball how she was getting along!"

Miss O'Leary smiled at Helen and Don and said, "Your daughter is a wonderful patient. Dr. Vidt told us about her before she came. He said she had made herself a world all her own."

The nurse straightened the crumpled sheet on Joy's bed, then went on: "She has faith in everything and everybody. She said she just knows Dr. Vidt's operation on her leg will be successful."

Joy stirred restlessly, but did not open her eyes.

"She'll be waking up soon now," Miss O'Leary said. "When she was going to sleep on the operating table, the last thing she said was, 'The sky above me is getting black, but I can still see the stars.' Dr. Vidt says he will never forget that!"

Joy soon began to move again. She kicked the sheet aside with her good leg. Before Miss O'Leary could put it back, Don and Helen saw the plaster cast on Joy's left leg; it extended from the knee all the way down to her foot.

"Reckon she's all right?" Helen asked in a trembling voice.

"Certainly," Miss O'Leary answered quickly. "All of these muscle and tendon grafting operations have to be put in a cast until they heal. She won't be wearing a cast very long."

"Daddy—"

Joy opened her eyes and looked around drowsily, but she couldn't stay awake. She closed her eyes again and said no more.

"That cast will protect Joy's leg while it's healing,"

Miss O'Leary explained. "Don't let the looks of it scare you."

"What's that row of little windows for?" Helen asked.

"They're there so Dr. Vidt can look at Joy's leg from time to time to make sure everything is all right," Miss O'Leary said.

Joy opened her eyes again and sighed, "Daddy, I've been asleep for a long time. If I can keep my eyes open, I'll tell you about my dream. My operation was wonderful! There was no pain, but I had a pleasant dream."

She lifted her head from the pillow and looked at her legs. She moved her good leg up and down.

"Don't try to move the leg that's in the cast," Miss O'Leary cautioned her. Then she said, "I'm anxious to hear about your dream!"

"It was night and there were thousands of stars in the sky," Joy said. She paused for a moment to collect her thoughts, then went on, "I saw mists rising up from the ground. Each cloud of mist turned into a white deer. There were as many of them as there were stars in the sky!

"The white deer began floating up toward the sky. Then I started to float up, too. We went up and up until we reached the meadows of the moon.

"Old Cracker was there, and he had his family with

him. And there were moon birds—just like my birds at the cliffs. They flew down and alighted on me. I'll always believe the meadows of the moon were real. I'd like to go back there!"

Dr. Vidt walked into the room and exclaimed, "Here you are, wide awake! How are you feeling?"

"Oh, just fine, Dr. Vidt," Joy said sleepily.

"She's just told us about her dream," Miss O'Leary explained. "She's been on the meadows of the moon with all her animal friends!"

"That must have been a wonderful dream," Dr. Vidt said. "I wish I could have a dream like that!"

"She's getting along all right, isn't she, Doc?" Don asked.

"Oh yes," Dr. Vidt replied enthusiastically. "Her operation went fine in every respect. She'll be walking soon."

"You don't know how glad I am to hear that, Dr. Vidt," Don said. He breathed a sigh of relief, then went on more briskly, "Well, I guess I'd better head for home now."

"Don't forget to take feed to the cliffs, Daddy," Joy said. "And tell Snowball the good news!"

Her father laughed and said, "Joyful, I'll tell him it won't be long before you can outrun him!"

"Wait a second, Don, and I'll walk with you to the elevator," Dr. Vidt said. "Miss O'Leary, I want you to take good care of our favorite patient. We've got to get her back home to Snowball as soon as we can! I'd like to keep her here with us, but she's missed back home by a lot of little folks."

∞

On the morning of June ninth, Joy's parents arrived very early. When they got to Joy's room, Helen began to gather Joy's clothes and other belongings and started putting them in her suitcase. Joy was ready to go home after six days in the hospital. She was already awake.

"Well, how's my girl this morning?" Don asked. "Ready to go home?"

"Yes, Daddy, but I'll miss Dr. Vidt and Miss O'Leary! They've been very nice to me."

"I know you'll miss them, and I'm sure they'll miss you, too."

"How's everything at home? How's Snowball?"

"Everything is just fine at home," Don replied. "Snowball sent you his greetings. He said he could hardly wait for you to get home."

Then Dr. Vidt came into the room. "Well, well! My friend Joy is leaving us today," he said with a smile. "We're going to miss what you've brought into this hospital!"

Joy looked rather puzzled.

"You brought us sunshine," Dr. Vidt explained. "We've got a lot of gloom in this hospital. Sunshine is always welcome to offset the gloom. You won't take all of your sunshine back. A little has rubbed off on us!"

Dr. Vidt, when will you come to see Joy?" Helen asked.

"I'll come about once a week until the cast is removed. If her leg starts hurting, let me know immediately. It might itch a little, but don't worry about that. The itching will just mean her leg is healing."

"We understand that, Dr. Vidt," Don said. "But will Joy have to lie in bed? Will she be allowed to walk while her leg is still in the cast?"

"She must take time to let her leg start healing," Dr. Vidt said. "I know she wants to be with her pets and get some sunshine, and I want her to do these things. But I also want her leg to heal properly."

Dr. Vidt turned to Joy and said, "I know you'll want to get out as soon as you can. But don't you take a step on that leg until I've removed the cast. I'll tell you when you can walk."

"Dr. Vidt, the first thing I want to do is to get Snowball out of the smokehouse," Joy said. "I want him outside again, and I want to play with him."

"It won't be long before you'll be able to walk and play with Snowball," Dr. Vidt assured her. "After that cast is off, the more exercise you get, the better it will be, and I'll explain to your mother and father how to massage your leg to stimulate growth."

"I'll tell Snowball what you've said, Dr. Vidt," Joy said. "I helped Snowball. Maybe he can help me!"

"If Snowball understands, I'm sure he'll help you," Dr. Vidt said.

"He'll understand," Joy said confidently.

"We want to thank you for taking such an interest in Joy, Dr. Vidt," Helen said.

"That's not only my duty," Dr. Vidt said quickly, "it's my pleasure, too." He paused, then added, "Your Joy is a fine girl."

Chapter Five

"We're home again!" Joy shouted ecstatically.

"Don't get too excited, Joy," Helen warned. "You mustn't try to climb out of the truck by yourself. We'll help you."

"Your mother's right, Joy. I'll carry you, and she can carry your suitcase," Don said as he climbed out of the truck.

Don walked around the truck, opened the door for Helen, and handed her the suitcase. Then he carefully lifted Joy out and carried her across the yard. Helen walked ahead to unlock the door.

Don carried Joy into her room and carefully placed her on her bed. She looked around the room and sighed contentedly.

"It's good to be home," she said softly.

Her father smiled down at her and said, "We're glad to have you back. We've been lonely here without you. Snowball has been lonely, too. Would you like to see him now?"

"Oh yes, Daddy! I can hardly wait to see him!"

"I'll fetch him from the smokehouse," Don said, and

hurried out of the room.

When Don returned, he was carrying Snowball in his arms. He set the fawn down beside Joy's bed. Snowball's eyes brightened when he saw Joy. He nudged at the bed and shook his head at her.

"Mind your manners, Snowball!" Joy said laughingly. "Have you missed me? I've missed you and all our friends."

"Snowball remembers you," Don said. "He was never that friendly with me when I fed him."

"Of course he remembers me, Daddy! We're good friends."

Snowball nudged Joy's face with his nose. She laughed and patted his head affectionately.

Hanging on the wall near Joy's bed was a large calendar. It had become very important in Joy's life. At the end of each day she crossed the day off. She was counting days when her mother came into the room.

"Daddy showed you where to put feed for my friends, didn't he?" Joy asked.

"Yes, we put the feed on their tables," Helen replied. "Chipmunks and squirrels came and ate, and birds flew in from all directions."

"Did you see Old Cracker?"

"Yes, and I fed him. He stood up on his hind legs and took the cracker in his front paws, then ate it."

"Did he whistle for you?"

"Yes, he did! Your father and I laughed at him until the birds wondered what was wrong with us!"

"Mama, I'm so glad you visited my Tomorrowland!"

"Tomorrowland? Is that what you call your place down by the cliffs?"

"Yes, I thought of that name while I was in the hospital. Do you like it, Mama?" Joy asked.

"It's a perfect name, Joy!" Helen exclaimed. "Your Tomorrowland is a very special place. I don't know why I've never gone there with you before."

"You and Daddy got to go and see my friends, but I have to lie in bed," Joy sighed.

"But you won't have to be in bed very long," Helen reassured her. "You'll be going back to see all your friends soon."

"Did any of my birds alight on you and Daddy?"

"Yes, some of them did."

Joy looked a little surprised, but said, "I'm so glad my friends accepted you! They accept people who are good and kind. There's a story about Saint Francis in one of my books. His birds loved him. He must have been a very happy man."

"I'm sure he was," Helen said. "There is no greater joy on this earth than to love and be loved by all living things."

"I wish I could have known Saint Francis and

helped him feed his birds," Joy said. "I wish I could see him now and invite him to go with me to my Tomorrowland. I'd like him to help me feed my birds, and I'd like to show him my chipmunks and lizards. I'll bet he'd love to see Old Cracker stand on his hind legs and whistle through his teeth for a cracker!"

"I heard what you said about Saint Francis and the birds," her father said as he walked into Joy's room. "I want to tell you another story about Saint Francis."

"When I was a boy, I was a good hunter. I was an excellent shot with any sort of gun. Then one day I read the same story you read and decided to stop hunting.

"I began to wonder if I could do what Saint Francis had done. First, I fed the chickadees in the snow. I wanted a bird to alight on me. I kept getting closer and closer to them, and finally a hungry chickadee with ice on his wings flew up and perched on my shoulder.

"I never killed another quail, dove, or grouse. And I also began to feed the wild animals. Some of them were almost starving. They became my friends, too.

"Then, before I married your mother, I got a job with a track repair crew on the C & O Railroad. I wanted to make some extra money during the winter months when there wasn't much to do on my father's farm. There were twenty men and a foreman in our crew, and we lived in camp cars here and there along the tracks. We were moved to the places where we were needed to repair the tracks. And I'll bet you can't guess what the fellows I worked with called me."

"I'll bet I can," Helen said.

"No, let Joy guess."

Joy thought for several seconds, then said, "I give up. What did they call you?"

"They called me the 'Bird Man.' And every man on that crew wanted to be able to do what I could do. While eating my lunch I could hold bread on my hand, and the hungry birds would fly in, alight on my arms, hands, and shoulders, and share my lunch with me. No other man in the crew could do that. They thought I had some sort of magic. All the magic I had was that the birds knew I wouldn't harm them."

"But Daddy, how did they know you wouldn't?" Joy asked. "How did they know Saint Francis wouldn't harm them? And how do they know we won't harm them when we go to Tomorrowland?"

"I can't answer that," her father replied. "But I'm sure they have their secret ways of knowing about people. I was the only man among the thousands who worked on hundreds of miles of C & O Railroad tracks in this area who could do that. Since I quit working for the C & O, I've seen several of the men I used to work with. They didn't remember my name, but they remembered my face and called me the 'Bird Man'."

"Mama, when did the birds first accept you?"

"When I married your father and came here to live, I went with him to feed the birds," Helen replied. "They accepted me because they had already accepted him."

"Then you were feeding the birds before I was born!" Joy exclaimed with astonishment.

"Yes, we were," her mother replied.

"Now I know why Daddy smiled at me at the hospital when he told me about the birds perching on his shoulders when he fed them for me," Joy said. "That must be why the birds have always accepted me—because of you two!"

"That's right," her father said. "Our influence lives after us. Look how long Saint Francis's influence has lived!"

Joy was looking out her window and wishing she could be outside when she saw a black car roll up to the edge of the yard and come to a stop.

"Mama, Mama!" she called excitedly, "Dr. Vidt is here!"

Helen hurried into the room and looked out the window.

"Now don't get too excited, Joy," she warned.

"I won't, Mama, but I know he's come to tell me about my leg. I want to get up from this bed as soon as I can!"

Just then there was a loud knocking at the door.

"Hurry, Mama! Go let him in!" Joy cried.

Helen went to the front door, and Joy heard her open it and greet Dr. Vidt.

"I thought I'd come to visit with my young friend awhile," Dr. Vidt said. "How is she?"

"She's just fine, Doctor," Helen replied.

"I thought she would be," Dr. Vidt said.

Joy lay in her bed and listened to her mother's conversation with the doctor. She turned her head toward the door. For a long time now, she had lain on her back and looked up at the ceiling.

"There you are!" Dr. Vidt exclaimed as he walked into Joy's room. "And you look just wonderful! You look as happy as ever!"

"Dr. Vidt, I'm so glad you've come," Joy said happily. "Why didn't you bring Miss O'Leary with you?"

"She couldn't come this time," he said apologetically, as he sat down in the chair beside Joy's bed.

"I've been thinking about Miss O'Leary," Joy said. "She was so nice to me while I was in the hospital!"

Dr. Vidt smiled and said, "If it weren't for Elsie O'Leary, I don't know what I'd do. She's worked for me so long she's more than a nurse—she's almost a doctor! I had to leave her at the hospital today so I could be free to come and see you."

He leaned over to examine the cast. He opened a window in it, removed some gauze, and looked at a place where he had transplanted muscle tissue.

"Do you suppose your friends down at the cliffs will remember you when you go back?" he asked. He rearranged the gauze and closed the little window in the cast.

"Yes, I'm sure they will," Joy replied.

"Who feeds your pets down at the cliffs now?" he asked.

"Mama," Joy replied. "Daddy doesn't have time now."

"Do the birds fly down to you, Helen?" Dr. Vidt asked.

"Yes, they fly in from all directions and alight all over me!"

"How do you account for that?" Dr. Vidt asked as he opened another window in the cast.

"They know I'm there to feed them," Helen explained. "They know I won't do them any harm."

"My parents are wonderful, Dr. Vidt," Joy said. "A long time ago my Daddy was a hunter. And when he was a hunter, all the birds and animals were afraid of him, but they don't fear him now."

"It must be wonderful to have wild birds and animals for your friends," Dr. Vidt said.

"Have you ever hunted rabbits and squirrels, Dr. Vidt?" Joy asked. "Have you ever hunted deer?"

"No, no, my dear girl," he assured her. "I've never had time. I've been too busy all my life. And I could never see a big man like me shooting a little bird, squirrel, or rabbit. That wouldn't be any fun for me. Anyway, I'm so big I'd scare all the animals and birds to death without having to shoot them!"

"Oh no, Dr. Vidt, you wouldn't scare them!" Joy said. "I know they'd like you! They'd be very friendly with you when they realized that you wouldn't harm them. Someday you can go and feed the animals down at the cliffs with me."

"I'd like that very much," Dr. Vidt said. "Now I've got to get back to the hospital. I've already stayed too long, but when I get here I always take my time. It's so peaceful and natural here. It's a wonderful place for a child to grow up."

"You'd love my Tomorrowland, Dr. Vidt!" Joy exclaimed. "It's a beautiful place and I'm sure all my friends would like you!"

"'Tomorrowland'—is that what you call your place down by the cliffs?" Dr. Vidt asked.

"Yes, it is," Joy replied.

The doctor smiled affectionately at his patient and said, "Well, you'll be able to go back to your Tomorrowland soon. Your leg is getting along fine. It won't be long until we can remove the cast and let you try walking on it."

"Without my crutches?"

"Yes, without crutches, but you'll have to use a cane

to steady yourself at first."

"Oh, I won't mind that," Joy said quickly. "How many more days will it be, Dr. Vidt?"

"I can't tell you the exact number of days," he replied.

"I hope I don't have to spend many more days in bed," Joy sighed. "Snowball has to stay in the smokehouse because I can't be out with him!"

"He won't have to stay there much longer. You'll soon be out walking with him," Dr. Vidt said. He stood up and stretched his arms toward the ceiling.

"I never have a pain, Dr. Vidt," Joy said. "I'm sure I'm going to get along all right."

"That's fine, Joy! Now, I'll be seeing you in a few days," he said. "Keep on getting better and say hello to Snowball for me."

Helen escorted Dr. Vidt to the front door. In a few minutes Joy heard him start his car and drive away. When she looked out her window, a cloud of dust was still hovering above the road.

After Dr. Vidt drove away, Helen went to the smokehouse, opened the door, and walked inside. She found Snowball munching wilted clover. When he saw Helen, he looked up and wiggled his ears. Helen laughed and reached down to stroke his face. She had become very fond of the little fawn. She put her arms around his neck and pulled him close. Snowball shook his head impatiently. He was hungry and he didn't want to stay in the smokehouse any longer.

"You want to be with Joy, don't you?" Helen asked.

When she took her arms from around his neck, Snowball ran out of the smokehouse into the yard. He kicked, jumped, and shook his tail. Then he dashed across the yard, leaped onto the porch, and began butting the screen door.

"Wait a minute and I'll let you in!" Helen said. She laughed and ran up the steps. "I know you want to be fed. Don't tear the screen out!"

She opened the door and the fawn ran inside. When Helen reached Joy's room, he was already drinking milk from his bottle.

"He's a wonderful pet!" Helen exclaimed breathlessly. "Maybe I should say he's a wonderful pest, but he is absolutely wonderful!"

"I heard you laughing, Mama," Joy said. "I'm glad you're getting to love Snowball more and more. You do love him, don't you, Mama?"

"I certainly do," Helen replied.

"Mama, you're changing."

"Why do you think so?"

"I used to think you didn't want Snowball in the house, but now I know you do. Of course, Snowball's home shouldn't be in the house, but he thinks he's part of the family."

Chapter Six

"Now, I'm not going to hurt you," Dr. Vidt said.

"I'm not afraid," Joy told him. "Today will be a day I'll always remember! After today, I'll have two feet and two legs!"

"Yes, but you'll have to learn to walk again," her father said.

"I'm going to walk, Daddy," Joy said positively. "I'll walk if it's the last thing I ever do. Don't worry about that!"

"That's the way I like to hear you talk," Dr. Vidt said as he took a small chisel out of his black leather bag. "Now I'm going to take that cast off."

Joy looked up at Dr. Vidt standing over her with the chisel in his hand. He looked like the smiling giant in Jack and the Bean Stalk. Then he began marking the cast with the chisel. He made a mark, then made a deeper mark in the same groove.

"Now, I'll have to soften this," he said. "This cast is almost as hard as one of the sandstones by your path, but I brought something with me that will help cut it, something that is softer than your hand. What do you think it is?"

"I don't know," Joy said.

"Just plain vinegar," the doctor said as he reached into his bag and took out a bottle filled with a brown-colored liquid.

"Now, Helen, I'll let you pour this," he told Joy's mother.

Mrs. Burton opened the bottle and poured a small amount of vinegar into the groove Dr. Vidt had made.

"That's enough right now," he said. Then he went to work again, making the trench deeper.

"Yes, Joy, this will be a great day for you all right," Dr. Vidt continued. "But they're all great days for you. You're a happy girl, aren't you?"

"Yes, Dr. Vidt," Joy replied. "Every day I live is a great day!"

Dr. Vidt stopped to rest. He smiled and winked at Joy.

"You've got a good place to grow up," he said. "You have forests and meadows to play in, and you have animals and birds for friends. You're a very lucky girl."

Then he went to work again, pushing the chisel up and down the length of the cast.

"You're also a very brave girl," he continued. "I don't think you know what being afraid is."

Dr. Vidt worked silently for a while, as his chisel cut deeper and deeper into the vinegar-soaked cast. He had his sleeves rolled up above his elbows, and his arms looked as large to Joy as the black oak saplings that grew by the cliffs.

"Pour more vinegar into the groove, Helen," he said as he wiped his brow.

"When will the chisel break through the cast?" Joy asked.

"It's almost through in one place, but I'll be careful. I won't hurt you."

"I'm not afraid, Dr. Vidt."

"There, it went through! Did you feel it?"

"No, I didn't," Joy replied.

"It won't take much longer now," Dr. Vidt said.

He worked slowly, using the chisel as a lever to pry on the cast.

"When I pry open a place big enough to get my hand in," he said, "I'll pull it apart all the way down."

Dr. Vidt tried to put his fingers into the small opening he had made.

"It's not big enough yet," he said. He picked up the chisel and carefully enlarged the opening.

"I'll try it again now," he said. "There—I've got a good hold."

Dr. Vidt pulled until Joy saw color come to his face, then she felt something give and heard a snap. The doctor laughed and held up the two pieces of the cast for her to see.

"It's off!" he said, as he dropped the pieces on the floor. "Now we'll have a good look at your leg."

"Can I sit up and look at my leg, too?" Joy asked excitedly.

"I see no reason why you can't."

Helen put two pillows against the headboard of the bed and helped Joy lift herself to a sitting position. She sat with her back and head against the pillows and watched Dr. Vidt remove the gauze from her leg.

"It looks good—very good!" Dr. Vidt said approvingly.

"When can I get up, Dr. Vidt?" Joy asked. "You know I've been a good patient. I haven't tried to get up and walk. I've done what you told me!"

"Right! You've been a good patient, so we'll let you stand up in just a few minutes. Look at that foot! Look how straight it is now!"

"It's as straight as my other one!" Joy exclaimed ecstatically. "Look at it, Mama! Look, Daddy!"

"Joy, I can't believe it," Helen said. "This is a miracle!"

"I thought your foot would never be straight again," her father said softly. He was so overjoyed he could hardly speak.

"Dr. Vidt, I'd like to stand up," Joy said positively. "I know I can! It's been a long time since I've stood up, but I'd like to try."

"All right, we'll do that very thing," Dr. Vidt said. "Then I want to show your parents how to massage your leg. The more physical therapy and exercise you have, the better it will be for you. We want the transplanted muscles to grow."

Dr. Vidt turned and walked out of the room. When he returned, he was carrying a cane.

"You'll probably need this at first," he said as he handed the cane to Joy. "Later you'll be able to put it away."

"What's that rubber thing on the end?" Helen asked. "I never saw a cane like that before."

"The rubber tip won't let it slip," Dr. Vidt explained. "She'll have less chance of falling. We don't want her to fall and hurt her leg."

"I'm ready to try now, Dr. Vidt!" Joy said eagerly.

"All right, put your feet down so you can feel the floor, but just sit there on the edge of the bed for a while."

Don and Helen helped Joy slide over to the side of the bed. Then she carefully lowered her feet to the floor. Helen put a pair of soft leather bedroom slippers on her feet.

"My feet feel like they've got pins and needles pricking them," Joy said.

"Now, just sit there a while," Dr. Vidt told her. "You've got to start slowly, but you'll be surprised at how fast you'll get better."

"It won't be too fast to suit me! I can't wait to walk with Snowball!"

"Now, stand up," Dr. Vidt said. "Put one hand on your Daddy's shoulder and one on mine. See how you feel standing up."

Dr. Vidt and her father helped her up.

"Bear your weight on your good foot and leg," Dr. Vidt told her. "Now, put your left foot down very gently."

Joy put her once-twisted foot down so it barely touched the floor.

"Wonderful! Wonderful!" Dr. Vidt exclaimed. "Do you think you can take a step if your father and I help you?"

"I'm sure I can!" Joy said proudly.

She was still standing between Dr. Vidt and her father with her hands on their shoulders. She took a deep breath and steadied herself. Then she very carefully took one small step.

"I did it! I can walk!" Joy said exultantly. "Let me take another step!"

"Let's not overdo this now," Dr. Vidt warned her.

"But it doesn't hurt! I won't bear much weight on this foot. It feels good! Honest it does!"

She took four more steps toward the door, then turned to her father and said, "Let's go outside!"

"Do you think you can walk that far?" Helen asked.

"I'm sure I can, Mama!"

"It's all right, Helen," Dr. Vidt said. "I won't let Joy hurt herself. Anyway, exercise is just what she needs right now."

They walked slowly through the living room and onto the porch. Helen saw a new light, brighter than ever before, come into her daughter's face. Joy breathed deeply of the summer wind and looked across the meadows toward her Tomorrowland.

Joy didn't go back to bed that afternoon. After Dr. Vidt left, she sat in a chair for a while to rest her leg. Soon, however, she decided she wanted to go to the smokehouse and feed Snowball. Helen handed her cane to her and helped her walk slowly across the yard to the smokehouse. Joy opened the door and looked inside.

"Just look at me, Snowball! I'm standing on both feet!" she said proudly.

Snowball looked up and blinked his eyes in the bright sunlight.

"I don't think he's noticed that I'm standing on both feet, Mama! Oh well—I'll just talk to him and pretend that he does!"

Just then Snowball caught sight of the bottle of milk Joy had brought him. He shook his head, flapped his long ears, and lunged at the bottle.

"Snowball, mind your manners!" Joy scolded. She

tried to look angry but laughed in spite of herself.

"You can't stay angry with him—he's too funny," Helen said. She was laughing, too.

"Open the door, Mama. Snowball and I want to go outside for a while," Joy said happily.

"You'll be as glad to get outside as I was, won't you, Snowball?"

Helen opened the door and Snowball bolted through it. He ran across the yard, kicking up his heels with glee. Suddenly he stopped and looked back at Joy, who was standing in the door of the smokehouse. He shook his head at her and pawed at the ground.

"Come on, Mama! Snowball's waiting for me," Joy said.

Leaning on her mother's shoulder for support, Joy hobbled slowly across the yard to Snowball. She stroked his face affectionately.

The summer wind was cool and soothing. She liked to feel the wind lift her ponytail and flutter the ends of the blue ribbon around it. After days of lying in bed, she was happy to be free again.

Joy had just opened her basket when her birds came down from the trees. They flew in from everywhere, like autumn leaves blown from the trees by the wind.

She leaned her cane against the rock and took feed from the basket, but the birds had not come for food.

They had come to welcome her home. They alighted on her shoulders and arms, and on the rock she used as a table. Others sat on the limbs of the trees and on the ground beneath them.

A few birds alighted on Snowball's back and a redbird perched on his head.

The rabbits were not afraid. They hopped up close to Joy. She had never fed the rabbits very much in the summer, because there was plenty of clover for them to eat. In the winter, though, it was different. When the clover and fescue grass were covered with snow, Joy took apples, carrots, and bread to Tomorrowland for them.

The chipmunks came running up with their tails arched over their backs. They were not afraid of the birds, the rabbits, or Snowball. But when Snowball tried to nudge one with his nose, the tiny chipmunk chattered indignantly and ran away.

"Snowball, do you know why all my friends are here today?" Joy asked as she spread grain over the gnarled beech roots. "They're here to welcome me back! They missed me!"

Just then Joy heard a familiar whistle, and looked around. She saw Old Cracker standing in the middle of the path.

"Oh, there you are," she exclaimed. "Where's your family?"

Then she saw Mrs. Cracker and her little ones waiting behind a cluster of wild gooseberry bushes. Joy took some crackers out of her basket and handed one to Old Cracker. Then she threw several crackers on the ground. When the four young ground hogs saw this, they abandoned their hiding place and came hurrying up to her. Mrs. Cracker soon joined the rest of the family.

Joy looked around at all the friends that had come to welcome her home. She stroked Snowball's face and said softly, "This is the happiest day of my life. I can walk without crutches and you can run like the wind. We're surrounded by friends who love us. What more could we want?"

Chapter Seven

"Mama, watch me! Watch me walk to the apple tree and back!"

"I've been watching you every day since Dr. Vidt removed the cast," Helen said.

"Mama, I can put my foot down easily," Joy said proudly. "It's getting better so fast, I'm beginning to think this leg and foot are normal, too."

Joy walked off without her cane. She tried to walk as if she had never used crutches or a cane.

"Joy, that's wonderful!" her mother exclaimed.

"Did you see how I put my foot down, Mama? Don't you think my limp is disappearing fast?"

"Yes, you hardly limp at all now."

"I've practiced walking in front of the mirror," Joy said. "That's why my limp is going away."

"Yes, your walk has improved, Joy," her mother said. "You don't have to show me. I watch you improve every day."

Joy walked up to Helen and stood facing her.

"Mama, I'm trying to show you I'll be able to do something I want to do very much," Joy said seriously.

"What's that, Joy?"

"I want to go to to Maxwell High School. I don't want to leave here. By September I'll be able to get on and off the school bus all right."

"You know I'd like you to stay here with us," her mother said. "But how would we get you to the school bus route? Your Daddy would have to take you in the morning and meet the bus in the afternoon. That means he'd have to get up earlier and work later. And what would we do with Snowball? Would he be content to stay here without you? He might try to get on the school bus with you!"

"Mama, I've been thinking about that," Joy said slowly. "Daddy could build a pen for Snowball."

"You've certainly been making plans, Joy!" Helen exclaimed. "Have you already picked a place for the pen?"

"Yes, I have, Mama," Joy answered quickly. "I know where Snowball finds the grass he likes, and there's a stream nearby. He'd have plenty of food and water."

"Do you think you can pass your classes at Maxwell High School?"

"You ought to know, Mama," Joy said. "You've taught me. What do you think?"

"I don't know about my teaching," her mother replied hesitantly. "I did my best with you, but…"

"Mama, I'm not afraid to go to Maxwell High

School," Joy interrupted. "If you and Daddy will let me go, I'll make passing grades."

∞

"Look, Daddy!" Joy shouted when she caught sight of her father coming home from the fields. She had been waiting for him. She left her cane leaning against the smokehouse and headed across the yard. Snowball followed close behind her. She walked to the barn, then turned around and started back.

"See—I can walk as well as anybody else!" she said proudly.

"You certainly can!" Don exclaimed. "Six months ago I would never have dreamed this could happen!"

"Daddy, I've been talking to Mama about something," Joy said. "I don't want to go away to school. I want to go to Maxwell High School."

"You know we want to keep you with us if we can," Don said. "But how would we get you to the school bus? And what will you do with Snowball?"

"You could build a pen that dogs couldn't get into, and we could keep Snowball in that!"

"That's an idea," Don said. "Where should I build it?"

"At the edge of the meadow by the stream," Joy replied.

"That would be a good place," Don said thoughtfully. "Snowball would have all the clover he could eat, and it would be easy to keep plenty of fresh water in his pen. A pen wouldn't be in the way there, either. You've thought of everything, Joy."

"I've tried to, Daddy," Joy said softly. "I want to stay here with you and Mama and Snowball."

Joy's father was deeply moved. He put his arm around her and said, "If that's what you really want, Joy, I'll do all I can to keep you here with us. I'll build a pen for Snowball, and I'll go see Reed Mennix, the Superintendent of County Schools, to see if he'll let you go to Maxwell High School. Don't worry—we'll work this out together."

July was a busy month for Don Burton. He harvested and sold all his sweet corn and used the money he got for it to buy wire for Snowball's pen. Then, during the busiest weeks of the summer, he somehow found the time to build a large, sturdy pen.

He cut locust posts and hauled them to the place Joy had chosen. He set each post in a deep hole and tamped dirt around it until it was as steady as a growing tree. Then he dug a ditch from post to post. He nailed the woven wire to the posts, placing one panel above another until it extended from the bottom of the ditch to the tops of the tall posts. Dogs could neither dig under nor jump over the fence.

Joy was standing beside the deer pen admiring her

father's work one afternoon when she saw his pickup truck coming down the road. Don Burton had been to Blakesburg to see Reed Mennix. Joy ran across the yard to meet him.

"Do you have good news, Daddy?" she asked breathlessly.

"It couldn't be better!" he replied. "Mr. Mennix told me your elementary work will be accepted!"

"Oh, Daddy, how wonderful!" Joy exclaimed happily. "Everything is working out all right for me!"

"You're already enrolled in Maxwell High School," her father said. "I have more good news, too."

"What is it, Daddy?" Joy asked excitedly.

"I won't have to take you to the school bus. A car will come to the house and take you to the bus in the morning and bring you back in the afternoon."

"Daddy, everything that's happened to me is good! I can walk without crutches or a cane, and I can stay at home and go to high school! I get to ride all the way to Maxwell High School and back!"

On September 6, Joy climbed out of bed long before daylight. She ate breakfast with her parents and gave Snowball his bottle of milk. Then she walked out to the deer pen with him .

"Snowball, I'm going to school today," she said cheerfully as she opened the gate. "You be good until I get back. There's plenty of clover in here, and there's fresh water for you to drink."

She put her arm around his neck and stroked his face. Then she closed the gate and carefully fastened it.

"Don't worry—nothing will harm you here," Joy said as she walked away. "I'll see you this afternoon."

When she got back to the house and walked into the kitchen, Joy asked, "Mama, I wonder what Maxwell High School will be like?"

"You'll soon know!" her mother said fondly.

Helen combed Joy's long blond hair into a ponytail and tied it with a blue ribbon. She would be wearing new clothes to high school on her first day. Her mother had already bought her clothes, books, and school supplies.

Joy was wearing a plaid madras skirt and a sleeveless cotton blouse. She had put on long blue socks and a new pair of brown loafers. She was standing in front of the mirror when her father walked into her room. He had put off his chores at the barn to come and see his daughter off to school.

"Isn't this something, Don?" Helen asked happily. "Our daughter is going to high school!"

"I'm wearing loafers, too!" Joy said, "and they're both the same size!"

"How pretty you are, Joy!" her father exclaimed.

"No one would believe you spent a whole year in

bed," Joy's mother added.

"That's the truth, Helen," Don said. He smiled broadly and winked at Joy. "What a good-looking girl we've got this morning! All dressed up and a good place to go! She's our high school girl this morning!"

"Be sure you don't forget the envelope on the dresser," her mother warned her. "Put it in your book bag and give it to your principal. I'm sending him your elementary grades."

"Mama, you taught me when I couldn't go to school. I didn't like it too well then, but now I'm glad you did. If it hadn't been for you, I wouldn't be going to high school this morning!"

Helen looked out the window when she heard a car drive up and sound its horn. "That's your ride, Joy," she said.

"I'll carry your books for you," her father said proudly. "Have you got everything?"

"Yes, Daddy—I've got my books, paper, and the envelope with my grades."

"Do you have your lunch money?" Helen asked.

"Yes, Mama."

The car waiting for Joy was an old model sedan with SCHOOL BUS printed on the side. The driver had a handlebar mustache and long gray hair. He was as large as Dr. Vidt and perhaps a little older. Joy climbed into the front seat and waved gaily to her parents and to

Snowball, who was watching her curiously. He pranced about, shook his head disgustedly, and butted the wire.

Don stopped cutting tobacco early that afternoon so he could be home when Joy returned. He wanted to know how she had liked her first day at school. Helen, too, was waiting eagerly for Joy to come home.

"There's the car," Helen said, just as Don walked into the kitchen. They both hurried out onto the porch.

"Maxwell High School is just great!" Joy shouted as she hurried across the yard.

"Were the other students nice to you?" her mother asked.

"They were wonderful, Mama," Joy replied happily.

"Do you think your leg is going to be all right?" Don asked.

"Yes, Daddy. It didn't get tired."

"Did you give Mr. Gallion the envelope?" her mother asked.

"Yes, Mama."

"Do you think you can pass all your classes?" Don asked.

"Yes, I'm sure I can," Joy replied proudly. "I wrote down everything my teachers told me to do. I have Mrs. Nottingham in English, Mr. Webber in history, Mr. Kenton in algebra, Taddie Sue Rockland in science, and Mr. Movius in Latin."

"Do you have classes upstairs?"

"I have two upstairs and two downstairs."

"Can you climb the stairs all right?" her mother asked.

"Yes, Mama, I can!"

"We've been lonely here today without you," her mother said.

"I missed you, too," Joy said. "And I missed

Snowball! Did you feed him at noon, Mama?"

"Yes, and I took feed to Tomorrowland, too," Helen replied.

"Tell us about your bus rides," Don said after they had walked into the house.

"I don't know the name of the man who comes to get me, but I'm going to call him Mr. Mustache. He took me to the Tiber River Road where we waited about two minutes for the big bus. The bus driver's name is Lonnie Brown—he has a nameplate. He gave me seat number 1, right behind him. Everybody is assigned to a seat and it's numbered. We line up by our seat numbers in the afternoon to get on the bus, so I'm first in line!"

"Oh—let me tell you something funny! This morning when I got on the big bus, a boy said, 'Good morning, Snowball.' At first I thought he knew about Snowball, and was naming me for him."

"No one knew my real name, so this afternoon when I got on the bus, I told Mr. Brown my real name is Joy. He told everyone my name, but someone said, 'Snowball's the name that suits her!'"

"Do they know about your pet deer?" her father asked.

"No, Daddy. They called me 'Snowball' because my hair is so blond."

Joy went outside to play with Snowball while her mother cooked supper. They walked down the path together toward Tomorrowland, and Joy told Snowball all about her first day at school just as if he were a human companion.

∞

"Mama, I don't think high school will be as hard as I thought," Joy said. She was reading her algebra book.

"I can help you with algebra and Latin if you like," her mother said.

"Thank you, Mama," Joy said, "but I don't believe I'll need any help."

Joy studied silently for a while. She was devoting all her attention to her algebra assignment. Finally she closed her book and sighed.

"Finished already?" Helen asked.

"Not yet, Mama. Mrs. Nottingham wants us to choose a subject and write a theme about it for Freshman English. There are so many things I'd like to write about, I can't decide on a subject."

"I can tell you what to write about," her mother said. "Remember the theme you wrote for me about Snowball? I gave you an 'A' on it. Rewrite that one and see if Mrs. Nottingham gives you an 'A', too."

"That's a good idea, Mama!" Joy exclaimed. "If I get an 'A' on that theme, I'll write more about Snowball and my friends in Tomorrowland."

∞

"Mama, my theme got an 'A'!" Joy shouted as she

ran into the kitchen the next afternoon. "And Mrs. Nottingham is reading it to all of her English classes!"

"I thought it was good," Helen said, "and I'm glad your English teacher agrees with me."

"Mama, my classmates want to know all about Snowball," Joy said. "They didn't know about him until I read my theme. Now everybody knows 'Snowball' is the name of my pet white deer, so no one calls me 'Snowball' anymore. They call me Joy."

You're getting along all right at Maxwell, aren't you?"

Mama, I believe I'm getting along better than anyone else in my class," Joy replied. "Mrs. Nottingham gave my theme to Mr. Gallion, our principal, and he asked me to come into his office after he'd read it. He asked me all about you and Daddy and Snowball."

Chapter Eight

One day in late September, when Joy had just come home from school, she left her books in her room and went out to the deer pen to take Snowball for his afternoon walk. Just as she started to open the gate, she heard a truck drive up and stop. She looked over her shoulder and saw a man in a green uniform getting out of the truck. He slammed the door and walked briskly toward the deer pen.

"Just a minute, Miss!" he said. "Let me see what you have in there!"

Joy closed the gate and turned around to face the stranger. When he came closer, she saw that he was wearing a holster attached to his belt. The handle of a revolver showed plainly.

"That's the first white deer I've ever seen," he said. "Where did you get it?"

"I found him in the woods," Joy replied suspiciously.

"In what woods?"

"In the woods down by the cliffs!"

"When did you find him?"

"Early last April."

"Where's your father?"

Joy looked curiously at the man. She wondered who he was and why he was asking her all these questions.

"He's in the barn hanging tobacco," she replied hesitantly. "If you want him, I'll go get him."

"Yes, I'll have to see him."

"There he is now," she said. Her father was walking toward them from the barn.

"Hello," Don Burton said as he shook hands with the stranger. "I'm Don Burton. Is there something I can do for you?"

"Yes, there is," the man said, opening his coat to show the badge pinned to his shirt. "My name is John Wilburn. I'm a state game warden, and I came to find out more about this deer you have in captivity here."

Joy's father was obviously stunned. He looked uneasily at the stranger's uniform and revolver. Don Burton did not allow anyone to carry a gun on his land unless he was an officer of the law.

"As you can see, Mr. Wilburn, we do have a pet deer," Don said coldly.

"It's against the law to keep a deer in captivity," the game warden said. "When I heard that you had one here, I came to see if it was true."

"People found out I had Snowball when I read my

theme about him for Mrs. Nottingham's English class," Joy said unhappily. "I wish I'd written about some other subject now."

"If you had, you couldn't keep this deer hidden very long anyway, young lady," the game warden said. "We would have found out you had him hidden here sooner or later."

"We're not trying to keep him hidden," Don Burton said quickly. "We keep him in this pen at night and whenever no one's here to watch over him. If we didn't, he wouldn't live a week. Because he's white, he'd be an easy target for hunters or predatory animals."

"Your daughter tells me she found him in the woods last April."

"She told you the truth," Don Burton said. "Did she tell you the condition he was in when she found him?"

"No I didn't, Daddy," Joy said.

"Well, I'll tell you, Mr. Wilburn," Don said. "His hip was broken and he couldn't walk. He would have died if she hadn't found him. She hopped all the way home on her crutches to tell us."

"On her crutches? Where are they now?" John Wilburn asked.

"Last spring she was on crutches," Don replied. "But thanks to God, a good doctor, and that white deer, she can walk without them now."

"What do you mean?" the game warden asked. "Do

you mean to tell me this deer helped her recover?"

"Yes I do," Don said. "I'm trying to tell you why we have the deer. We really didn't know it was against the law to have a pet deer. The only reason we have him in this pen is to protect him from dogs and hunters. When he was crippled, we kept him in her room in the house."

"You kept this deer in your house?"

"Yes, we put his leg in splints and put him in a sling that we hung from the ceiling to keep the weight off his legs until his hip healed," Don explained. "At first I didn't think we could save him, but Joy convinced me to go to Auckland and get Dr. Martin, the veterinarian. He came, but he didn't think the deer had a chance, either. He wanted to put him to sleep.

"But Joy begged him to save the deer, so he finally agreed to do what he could. We cut holes in the ceiling and put ropes around the joists to hold his sling up. Joy fed him from a bottle. She was sure he'd get well and walk again!"

"And you did too, didn't you, Snowball?" Joy interrupted.

"That's an interesting story, but you still haven't told me how the deer helped your daughter recover," John Wilburn said.

"Soon after this deer had recovered, Joy's doctor came to see her. He wanted to operate on her leg and foot," Don said. "My wife and I were a little nervous about the whole thing, but Joy wasn't. She had seen this deer walk again after breaking his hip, and she was sure that she would walk again, too. As you can see, the operation was a success.

That white deer gave Joy the faith and confidence she needed."

"Your story is a little hard to believe, Mr. Burton," John Wilburn said. "It's almost as fantastic as the one a fellow named Alec Robinson told me when I went to get his pet fox. When I told him he'd have to turn it loose, he said he was afraid his fox would follow some dog home and be mistaken for a fox with rabies. He was afraid some farmer would shoot him. I never got over that one! A fox following a dog home! Every time I think of that story, I have to laugh!"

"Everything I've told you is the truth," Don Burton said coldly. "Show this suspicious officer the scar on your leg, Joy."

Joy pulled down the long sock that concealed her scar.

"Why, you have had an operation on your leg!" the game warden exclaimed. He was obviously surprised to discover that Don Burton had been telling the truth.

"Dr. Vidt grafted new muscle tissue there," Joy explained. "My leg is growing, now. Mama and Daddy have to massage it and I have to get a lot of exercise.

Snowball and I get our exercise together."

"I can see that you've become very attached to this deer," John Wilburn said. "But the law is the law, and it's my job to enforce it."

"You don't mean you're going to take Snowball away?" Joy cried. "You can't do that, Mr. Wilburn!"

"Keeping a deer in captivity violates a state law, young lady. I'm sorry, but I can't make an exception for you."

"He can't take you away from me, Snowball!" Joy said protectively. Snowball was prancing about restlessly in his pen.

"I will not allow you to take this deer," Joy's father said firmly.

"Do you know, Mr. Burton, that you are openly defying a state game law?" the game warden asked. "Do you want to read the law? Do you know you can be arrested for what you're doing?"

He took a book of state game laws from his inside coat pocket.

"No, I don't want to read the law, Mr. Wilburn! If I can keep you from taking this deer, I'll do it! I'll go to town to see an attorney tomorrow!"

"That will just be a waste of time and money," the game warden said. "The law is on my side."

"Aren't you supposed to protect wild game, Mr. Wilburn?" Joy asked.

"Yes I am, Miss," he replied. "That's what I'm doing here. Wild animals shouldn't be kept in captivity."

"Do you hunt?"

"Yes, I do some hunting," the warden replied. "But I don't have much time to hunt—I'm too busy arresting those who break the game laws!"

"You mean killing wild animals and birds is protecting wildlife?" Joy asked angrily.

"What's wrong with hunting?" the game warden asked.

"We don't kill any wildlife and we don't allow anyone to hunt on this farm," Don said. "If you take that deer from us, what are you going to do with him?"

"I'll take him back to the nearest game reserve. He'll be much happier with his own kind."

"He'll never stay there," Don said.

"We'll give him a chance and see," John Wilburn said. "I'll be here Saturday to see what your lawyer has told you. If we have to, we'll take court action to get this deer!"

Joy opened the gate and Snowball rushed out into the yard. When Joy called to him, he stopped, wiggled his ears, and walked back to her. Together they walked slowly across the meadow toward Tomorrowland.

"Your daughter knows how to handle him," the game warden said. "I never saw a deer as tame as that one!"

"The other wild animals and birds are that tame with her, too," Don said. "Birds light on her shoulders and arms and eat out of her hands."

"You don't expect me to believe that, do you? Birds wouldn't trust anyone that far!" the warden scoffed.

"I know better than that," Don said.

"Well, I'd have to see birds lighting on your daughter before I'd believe it, Mr. Burton. Your stories remind me of Alec Robinson's fox story."

"You won't be able to see it."

"That's what I thought! Why not?"

"They'd be afraid of you."

"It sounds like a tall tale to me."

"But it's not."

"Then why couldn't I see it?"

"Because you carry a gun."

"Have you ever seen this happen?"

"Yes, many times," Don replied. "And the birds have perched on me and my wife Helen while we were feeding them, too."

John Wilburn shook his head and said, "I don't think I understand this. But I'll be back Saturday. Maybe I'll find out more then."

When Joy came home from her walk that afternoon, she went inside and sat by the fireplace with her parents. She watched the flames lick over the huge logs and leap up the chimney.

"Mama, did you see the game warden?" she asked.

"I saw him, but I didn't go out," Helen replied. "I was suspicious of him when I saw his uniform and gun."

"I'm not going to let him take that deer," Don said.

"What did you finally tell him, Daddy?"

"I told him that he couldn't take Snowball if I could help it."

"How can we help it?" Helen asked. "He says there is a state law against our keeping Snowball for a pet."

"I'll go to Blakesburg and see Oscar Timmons," Don said. "He's the best lawyer in town. Maybe he can help."

"Daddy, I can't give Snowball up!" Joy said. "I'll put him in the smokehouse and lock the door!"

"Locking him in the smokehouse won't help," her father said. "We've got to fight the law with the law."

"Maybe Oscar Timmons can find a way," Helen said hopefully.

"I'd like to wake up in the morning and learn that all of this was just a bad dream," Joy sighed.

"We saved the deer's life and now a game warden wants to take him away from us," Don said. "He would've died in a few more hours if we had left him in the woods!"

"I can't give him up! I've never had a fight in my life, but I'll fight to keep Snowball!" Joy declared.

Her father got up to put a log on the fire. It rolled

down onto the hearth and little clouds of smoke rose toward the ceiling. He took the long tongs from a nail and lifted the log back into place. Then he took a whisk broom and swept the smoking coals back into the fireplace.

"We'll do everything we can to keep Snowball," he said. "John Wilburn will soon find out we don't give up easily!"

"I hope Oscar Timmons can help us," Helen said.

"If the state game law is against us," Don said, "there's not much Oscar can do. But I'm not sure the law is against us. That game warden might have been bluffing."

"Joy, you have to get up early in the morning," Helen said. "Your school bus comes early. It's time for you to go to bed."

"I hope I dream this isn't true!" Joy said unhappily.

∞

When Joy came home from school the next afternoon, she let Snowball out of his pen and took him to Tomorrowland. When they returned, it was very late and darkness was hovering over the land. Her parents had eaten supper and her mother had already prepared Snowball's bottle of milk.

"You stayed late," her father said.

"Yes, Daddy, I did. We've been watching the dead leaves float by on the Little Sandy River. I forgot about the time until it started getting dark."

"Sit down and eat your supper now, Joy," her mother told her. "I'll feed Snowball. Your Daddy can tell you what happened in Blakesburg."

"Is it good news, Daddy?" Joy asked hopefully.

"Eat something before I tell you," he said. "Eat while I tend the fire." He went into the living room.

Joy sat down and ate her supper hurriedly. As soon as she had finished, she hurried into the living room and sat down before the blazing fire with her father.

"I was afraid you wouldn't eat, Joy, if I told you what I found out from Oscar Timmons first," he told her.

"Then it's bad news, Daddy?"

"I'm afraid so," Don replied.

"What did Mr. Timmons say?"

"He said the law was on the game warden's side. He read the law to me and I told him our story."

"What will we do now? Will we let the game warden take Snowball?"

"Not if we can help it!"

"What advice did Mr. Timmons give you?" Joy asked.

"He said the law was on the game warden's side, but the law of the heart was on our side. He said for us to try to think of a way to keep the deer."

Joy frowned, but said nothing. She sat silently for

awhile, watching the flames dance about in the fireplace. Suddenly she looked up at her father and smiled. She had thought of something she could do to protect Snowball.

Chapter Nine

Promptly at nine on the next Saturday, Helen heard someone rapping on the door. She left her baking and hurried out of the kitchen. When she opened the door, she recognized the game warden.

"Ma'am, I'm John Wilburn," he said.

"Yes, I know," Helen said coolly.

"You're Mrs. Burton, aren't you?"

"Yes."

"I've come to take the white deer. It's not in the pen."

"Is that your pickup truck out there with the pen on it?" Helen asked.

"Yes, Ma'am. I'll take him back to the game reserve in that."

"I hate to see my daughter's pet being taken away from here in that truck," Helen said. "You're sure you can take our deer, aren't you?"

"Yes, I am! It's the law."

"Everything's on your side but the deer! He belongs to us!" Helen said angrily.

"I didn't come here to discuss this with you, Mrs.

Burton," the game warden said. "I've come to see your husband. Where is he?"

"He might be out at the barn, or he might be harvesting corn or digging potatoes. I don't know just where he is. You'll have to find him yourself."

"Do you know where the deer is?"

"No, I don't."

"Is your daughter here?"

"I don't see her, do you?"

"I'd like to look inside the house, Mrs. Burton!"

"Show me your search warrant first!" Helen demanded.

"I don't have one," Wilburn admitted.

"Then you don't come in!"

"If that deer is on this place, I'll find him before sunset," the game warden said angrily.

"No one is stopping you," Helen said. She smiled, then added, "No one will be helping you, either."

"I can see I'm not going to have any cooperation," the officer said, "but your attitude will just make me even more determined to take the deer!"

"I don't doubt that, Mr. Wilburn," Helen said emphatically. "But you're wasting your time standing here talking to me! Go find Don! Go find the deer! Go! I smell something burning on the stove!"

"All right, then! I will go, and I will find that deer!"

When Helen looked out the window a few minutes

later, she saw John Wilburn standing by the deer pen. He was looking for Snowball's tracks. An hour later, when she was out on the porch, she looked toward the bluebirds' apple tree and saw him walking alone up the path toward his truck. A few minutes later he drove away.

At about six Helen and Don sat down to supper without Joy. They were interrupted a few minutes later by someone knocking on the door.

"It's John Wilburn," Helen sighed. "That's the way he knocks. You go to the door!"

"Oh, it's you, Mr. Wilburn," Don Burton said as he opened the door.

"I was here this morning, but I couldn't find you," the game warden said. "I talked to your wife, but she wasn't very friendly."

"You won't find friendship here as long as you try to take Snowball," Don said.

"What did you find out from your attorney?"

"In regard to that question, Mr. Wilburn, I have nothing to say," Don replied coldly.

"I walked all over your farm this morning," the game warden said. "I never saw you, your daughter, or the deer. I couldn't find any fresh tracks, either, but I followed that path down to some large rocks where I found plenty of old tracks."

"Where do you suppose the deer is?" Don asked.

"In this house," John Wilburn replied.

"He's not in this house!"

"I don't believe you!"

"Come in and search the house, then," Don said, stepping aside.

"All right, I'll accept that invitation."

John Wilburn looked under the beds, behind the curtains, and even behind the sofa that was backed up close to the wall. He searched every place big enough to hide even a rabbit for the white fawn. When he went into the kitchen, Helen, who was still sitting at the table, did not speak to him.

"Your daughter and the deer are both missing," Wilburn said. "They must be together."

"But where?" Don asked.

"I'd like to know," the game warden replied. "And I'll find out, too!"

"Maybe you will," Don said. "But maybe you won't!"

"Someone is helping you hide this deer, and that is breaking the law! We can arrest him as an accessory!"

"Now don't get suspicious again, Mr. Wilburn," Don said. "You searched the house and didn't find the deer, did you?"

"No, but you're breaking the game laws of this state. You may have some clever tricks up your sleeve, but I assure you, I'll find that deer!"

"You know, the deer could be back on the game reserve," Don said.

"I can check on that. The trees will be bare soon and a white deer won't be hard to find!"

"But when the snow falls," Don said, "he'll be very hard to find!"

"I can't get anywhere with you, either," John Wilburn sighed.

"Not when you're trying to take away the greatest joy our daughter has ever had! That deer would've been a handful of dust if she hadn't found him. She saved his life."

"Don, sit down and eat your supper before it gets cold," Helen said. "Don't argue with him. He doesn't understand and he never will, because he hasn't been through what we have. If he has so much confidence in himself, let him go find that deer!"

John Wilburn glared at them and his face grew red. "I'm not through," he said angrily. "I promise you I'll be back!"

On this moonless September night, millions of stars illuminated the sky. The trees and cliffs stood out in bold relief against the semi-darkness of early evening.

Joy and Snowball walked slowly and cautiously toward Tomorrowland. The chipmunks were asleep in their homes under rocks and in holes in the ground. Old Cracker, too, had led his family away to their den. Tomorrowland was deserted and silent except for the occasional hooting of an owl.

Joy and Snowball walked over a carpet of leaves too wet with dew to make a rustling sound. Soon they reached the well-worn path that led from Tomorrowland to the Burtons' home.

Helen and Don were standing on the front porch anxiously awaiting their daughter's return. Suddenly Helen cried, "Look, Don! She's coming—along the path by the apple tree!"

Don could see a white object moving slowly toward them through the darkness. Joy was bringing Snowball home.

October came, bringing cold winds from the north. Each clear, cool night threatened to bring frost.

Joy kept Snowball in her room at night. She was afraid that John Wilburn would pull the lock off the smokehouse door and take him. She knew that the game warden wouldn't dare break into her room, and it wasn't likely that he would get a search warrant to search their house again.

While Joy was at school, Snowball stayed with her father. Don took the tame young deer with him every morning when he went to work on the farm.

One morning, when Don saw Snowball chasing the chickens, he clapped his hands and shouted. The startled deer jumped and ran away from the loud noise. Soon he forget his fear and returned, but his quick getaway gave Don an idea.

That evening Don told Joy he was afraid the game warden would make another attempt to catch Snowball soon. Don was afraid Wilburn might try to catch Snowball when he was out walking with Joy in the afternoon.

"Joy, you're going to have to be very careful," Don said. "Don't let Snowball wander away from you. If you see the game warden, clap your hands and scream 'scat!' Snowball will run like the wind! No one could catch him!"

At about two o'clock on a warm October afternoon, Don Burton was in the field husking corn, and Snowball was lying down nearby. The warm autumn sun made him very drowsy.

Suddenly Don heard a noise above the rustling of the dry corn husks. He looked up and saw John Wilburn hurrying toward Snowball with a lasso in his hand. Don clapped his hands and screamed "scat!" Snowball scrambled to his feet, leaped over the pile of corn stalks, and ran away as fast as he could.

"Nice trick, Mr. Burton," John Wilburn said sarcastically.

"You almost got him this time," Don said, "but he got away!"

"You've trained that deer very well! I should arrest you!"

"For what?"

"For holding onto that deer—keeping him in captivity!"

"Look at that white speck in the distance," Don said. "Is that keeping an animal in captivity? I'd call that freedom! Look!"

"I still feel like arresting you!"

"Arrest me then," Don said indifferently. "You know it'll be a false arrest."

"You're right. I can't arrest you now, but I'll be back again. Don't you doubt that, Mr. Burton!"

On the second Saturday in October, Joy awoke and got dressed long before dawn. She filled a basket with feed for her birds and animals, prepared a bottle of milk for Snowball, and packed some sandwiches for herself. By daybreak she and Snowball were ready to leave.

"I have a feeling the game warden will be here today," her father warned her. "He's upset over his failures and he wants to capture Snowball so he can show him to people."

"I've told my friends at school about this," Joy said. "What do they think?"

"They think we're right," she replied.

"I'm glad they feel that way."

"I'll go to the Little Sandy today," Joy said. "There is a carpet of leaves from the cliffs to the river, so we won't leave any tracks!"

"Remember to clap your hands and scream 'scat' if you see John Wilburn," her father reminded her.

"I'd better get going before he comes," Joy said as she opened the door.

When Joy and Snowball reached the cliffs, the birds were just beginning their day. They were singing merrily and fluttering from tree to tree. The Little Sandy River was almost covered with leaf-ships sailing slowly by. Their red, brown, and yellow sails gleamed in the first rays of the morning sun.

Joy spread chick feed on the flat tops of the big stones for the birds and on the tops of the smaller stones for the chipmunks. She gave the Cracker family their crackers, and spread shelled corn on the beech roots for the gray squirrels. Then she gave Snowball his bottle of milk. Finally, after every bird and animal in Tomorrowland had been fed, she sat down and ate a sandwich.

When Joy finished eating, she noticed that there were only four birds on the stone table. All the others had flown up into the trees without finishing their meal. Suddenly, the chipmunks scampered off, and the gray squirrels ran up the trees to their dens.

"Scat!" Joy screamed at Snowball, and clapped her hands as loudly as she could.

Snowball leaped high into the air, and bounded up the path toward home. Joy had not seen anyone, but she knew there was an intruder in Tomorrowland. She looked around quickly and saw John Wilburn standing behind her.

"Who told you to come here?" Joy demanded angrily.

The game warden didn't answer. He was too angry to speak. His fists were clenched tightly at his sides and his face was very red.

"Don't you know you shouldn't be here with a gun?" Joy asked.

Wilburn still did not move or speak.

"Why don't you speak up?" Joy asked, after waiting for a reply. "Is it because you didn't get Snowball?"

The warden remained silent, and his lips trembled.

"My friends warned me!" Joy said. She took a step toward the game warden. "And I warned Snowball! My friends told me there was an unwelcome visitor here!"

Still he did not speak to her.

"Are you ill?"

"No, no," he replied.

"Can I help you?" Joy asked.

"Where did the deer go?" the game warden asked.

"I can't say for sure," Joy said, smiling sweetly.

"What power do you have over birds and animals?"

"They aren't afraid of me because they know I won't harm them. They trust me."

"I saw the animals eating with the birds, too. How do you get them to do that?"

"They're not afraid of the birds or of me."

"This is all very strange," John Wilburn said.

Joy wondered why the game warden's lips trembled as he turned and walked away. She knew that he was gone when the birds and animals returned. Soon she saw Snowball bounding back down the path toward her.

Chapter Ten

"If John Wilburn was so scared he couldn't speak, he might never come again," Joy's mother said hopefully. "We might be through with his snooping around here and..."

"Wouldn't that be great, Mama?" Joy interrupted. "Snowball would like that—he doesn't like our screaming 'scat' at him. He's afraid. He likes Tomorrowland, where we don't have fear."

"Wouldn't we all like to live without fear?" Helen asked reflectively. "Who would believe that saving a deer's life would cause all this trouble?"

Joy stroked Snowball's face gently. She was planning to take him to Tomorrowland.

"Do you think the game warden will be back after what happened Saturday?" Helen asked Don.

"That fellow will be back! He'll keep coming back, too. John Wilburn has never worked as hard in his life to get an animal as he'll work now to get Snowball!"

"Surely not so soon after Saturday!" Helen said.

"He'll try to take us by surprise," Don said. "That's the way I've got him figured."

"You can see almost to the cliffs now that the leaves have fallen off the trees," Joy said. "You watch me until I get out of sight. After I get to the cliffs our friends will warn us if the game warden comes near."

"I'm worried about John Wilburn," her father warned. "He's tried four times to get Snowball. Watch out! He'll really make an all-out effort next time!"

"Daddy, I need to walk with Snowball," Joy said. "I've been on busses and going from room to room and reciting all day!"

"Don, you're too suspicious," Helen said. "I think it'll be all right for her to take Snowball for a walk."

"Let's hope I don't have to shout 'scat,' Snowball," Joy said as she walked out onto the porch with him.

They walked down the little path that wound back and forth through the woods, but the birds and animals didn't come to greet them.

"A few more steps, Snowball, and our friends will come," Joy said softly.

She and Snowball went deeper into Tomorrowland, but there wasn't a sign of life. She stopped to look around, but didn't see anything wrong.

"Well, Snowball, what do you think of this?" she whispered.

Suddenly two men rushed from behind two large stones at the edge of the path. They pulled a net taut across the path, but Joy didn't see this movement until

144

it was too late. When she clapped her hands and shouted, Snowball leaped into the net.

"Oh, Snowball!" she screamed. "They've got you!"

"I said I'd be back," John Wilburn said. "Don't be afraid, Miss. We won't hurt you. We're after this white deer."

"Snowball is mine," Joy sobbed. "You can't have him!"

"No, he belongs to the state," Wilburn said.

The two game wardens pulled the net in close around Joy and Snowball, as the fawn jumped about wildly inside the net. The wardens had stretched the net along the sides of the path and directly across it. After Joy and Snowball had walked in, the game wardens had closed the net behind them.

Joy had her arms around Snowball's neck as the game warden Joy didn't know reached in and grabbed Snowball by his long ears. John Wilburn pulled a rope from his pocket and tied it around the fawn's slender neck. Snowball kicked and butted furiously but could not escape.

"John, he's not a strong animal," said the stranger.

"You can't have my deer!" Joy cried repeatedly.

The men, still busy with the net, worked on, as if they didn't hear her.

"Fold the net, John," said the stranger. "Leave the deer to me. I'll handle him."

145

John Wilburn, smiling happily, unfastened the net from the trees and rolled it into a neat bundle. Snowball jumped about and shook his head wildly.

"He's never been tied before," Joy said.

"He's tied now," the strange warden said. "He won't get away, so he might as well hold still. I could carry him a lot easier if he didn't jump around so much. I'm afraid he might hurt himself on this rope!"

He pulled the struggling deer toward him, then picked him up and held him in his arms.

"Man, is he scared! His heart's beating like a triphammer!"

"You're free to go home and tell your father I've got the white deer," Warden Wilburn said proudly. "Your signal didn't work this time! The sooner you can stop crying, the better it will be for you. You don't know how lucky you are to have your father at home with you and not in jail for keeping this animal in captivity."

"I wish Daddy were here," Joy sobbed. "He said you'd be back and try something new."

"Miss, I figured it all out Saturday. You can tell your father that."

The two men soon left the path and walked in the direction of the road. Snowball kicked and struggled at first, but soon gave up and submitted to being carried. Joy stood in the path and watched the game wardens carry Snowball into the dense grove of white oaks near the road. When she could no longer see them, she started home to tell her parents what had happened.

∞

When Helen looked out the window and saw Joy running up the path alone, she knew something was wrong. She hurried out of the house and called Don, who was working at the barn. Together they ran down the path to meet Joy. Between sobs, she told them what had happened and in which direction the two game wardens had gone.

"They've parked their truck somewhere along the road," her father said. "They went through the woods to the cliffs and have gone back to their truck the same way. They worked all this out before they set the trap!"

"Daddy, won't I ever see Snowball again?"

"Yes, in a very few minutes," Don replied quickly. "We're going to follow that truck! Now dry your eyes and let's go!"

Don, Helen, and Joy hurried over to the truck and climbed inside. Don drove faster than he ever had before, and they soon saw a cloud of dust hovering in the air in front of them.

"They're gone!" Don said. "They're on their way!"

"Where to, Daddy?"

"We'll soon find out!"

"We're gaining! The dust is getting thicker now," Helen said.

When they reached the top of the next hill, Joy shouted with glee. John Wilburn's truck was just ahead. Snowball was in a pen on the back of the truck.

"I wish that truck would break down!" Helen said vehemently.

Just before they reached the Tiber Road, the game warden's truck slowed down, then stopped. Don stopped, too. John Wilburn stepped out and walked back to the Burtons' truck.

"Why are you following us?" he asked.

"We're going to see where you take him," Don replied coldly.

"So you can steal him back?"

"We don't have to steal him! He'll come back home! I don't think he'll enjoy this freedom you've been talking about!"

"He won't come back to you! He won't want to come back after he gets with his own kind. He'll be happy among them. The other officer is an Ohio game warden, and we're taking the fawn to the McKinley Game Reserve. There's no need for you to follow us."

"But there's no law against it, so we're going to," Don said firmly. "We want to see that Snowball reaches his new home!"

Warden Wilburn glared at Don for a moment, then walked back to his truck. Soon the warden's pickup was rolling down the Tiber Road with the Burtons' truck

149

close behind. Both trucks crossed the bridge over the Ohio River and headed down the road which led to the McKinley Game Reserve.

Soon John Wilburn turned off onto a lonely road that led into the forest, and Don followed. When Wilburn stopped his truck, Don stopped close behind him and Joy scrambled out and ran to the warden's truck. She reached up to the pen and rubbed Snowball's nose through the slats.

Suddenly she heard something behind her. She turned around and found herself standing face to face with a deer. Three other deer were standing nearby.

"Now, Mr. Burton, you see we're not trying to keep your deer!" John Wilburn said emphatically. "We've brought him back to his own kind, where he belongs!"

"But you belong to me, don't you Snowball?" Joy said as she stroked his face between the slats. Then she turned to the strange deer and said, "You'll look after Snowball for me, won't you, and be his friend? He needs you!"

When John Wilburn opened the door of the pen, Snowball sprang forward like a wild rabbit. He kicked up his heels and ran away from the wardens and their pen as fast as he could. Suddenly he stopped and looked around. When he realized that he was in a strange place, he turned around and hurried back to Joy.

While Snowball was standing beside Joy, the closest

deer came up and rubbed noses with him. Then the three other deer came forward and made friends with the fawn.

"He'll be happy here," John Wilburn said.

"You feel very proud now, don't you?" Helen asked angrily.

"I feel relieved now," the warden replied. "I can go home and sleep tonight."

"You'll probably get a raise in salary," Don said contemptuously.

Snowball's meeting with his own kind seemed to be a pleasant one until the Burtons started home. Then he seemed to have decided that the Burtons were his own kind, for he put his front feet on the running-board as if he were trying to get into the truck with them. Then he jumped down, and they drove away.

"I feel better now, knowing Snowball is with his own kind," Joy said. "But I hate to go home without him. He's like one of our family."

"Mama, what happened yesterday is like a bad dream," Joy said at breakfast. "I can't believe it really happened. This is the first morning since last April, except when I was in the hospital, that I've not fed Snowball. There can't be much grass where he is now. I wonder what he's finding to eat?"

"There's no fence around the game reserve," her

father said. "He'll be home for breakfast one day soon!"

"But when he gets off the game reserve, he'll be in danger," Helen said. "He's not afraid of people, and somebody might shoot him!"

"Yes," Don replied. "That could happen. I hope not!"

"Oh, I hope he'll get back safely if he tries to come home!" Joy said unhappily.

On Wednesday morning, Joy awoke early. She was used to getting up when her parents did so she could eat with them, feed Snowball, and be ready when Mr. Mustache came for her.

"If Snowball were here, everything would be all right," she said to her father and mother at the breakfast table. "I dreamed about him last night. In my dream we were running races on the meadow. Then Snowball started chasing a ball of milkweed furze blowing in the wind. When the wind lifted the ball high in the air, Snowball climbed up invisible stairsteps and batted the ball back with his front hoof. He turned there, high in the wind, and ran back down the steps to get the ball. I woke up laughing!"

"Snowball is thinking as much about you as you are about him," Don said. "He might have escaped already and may be trying to find his way back home!"

"Oh, I hope so!" Joy exclaimed.

Soon she heard Mr. Mustache drive up and sound his horn. She grabbed her books and hurried out the door.

On this rainy morning, the darkness lingered, but it gradually faded into a murky light. Joy looked from her bus window at the barren trees. Their branches had been picked clean by the lean fingers of an autumn wind.

Thursday and Friday passed slowly. The cold autumn rain continued to fall. Each morning and afternoon Joy looked out her school bus window at the dark hills and barren trees. This was a time of great loneliness for her.

On Saturday morning, November 16th, Joy awoke early but didn't get out of bed. She knew this would be still another long, lonely day. Many days had passed and Snowball had not returned. Joy wondered if he were happier on the game reserve with his own kind than he had been with her.

After breakfast, she went out to the barn to take her father the hot coffee her mother had made for him. He was stripping tobacco, and the morning was damp and cold. On her way back to the house, she heard two hounds chasing a fox. The hounds were in the white oak grove and she could tell that they were coming toward her. She looked down the path, thinking she might see the fox cross the meadow ahead of the dogs.

Suddenly she saw a flash of white among the trees. It was Snowball! The dogs were chasing him! He leaped over a clump of wild blackberry briars and came running up the path, with the two hounds, one black and tan and the other blue-speckled, only a few yards behind him!

"Snowball!" Joy screamed. "Mama, it's Snowball! Daddy, Daddy, it's Snowball! Daddy, come quick!"

Neither Don, who was inside the barn stripping tobacco, nor Helen, who was in the house doing her chores, could hear Joy's screaming. She realized she had to act quickly. Snowball had seen her and was running to her for protection!

"Daddy!" she screamed as loudly as she could.

"If only he could hear me!" she thought. "If Mama would only look out the window!"

"Daddy!" she screamed again. "Mama!"

Joy looked around quickly, hoping to see something she could use as a weapon. She caught sight of a hickory hoe handle leaning against a post in the deer pen. She ran for it as fast as she could. Snowball and the hounds were very close now.

"Get away from him!" she shouted as she grabbed the hoe handle. "Get! Leave him alone!"

The hounds paid no attention to her. They had been trained to kill. As Joy rushed forward to meet them, Snowball ran past her at breakneck speed. Joy heard him crash into the fence, but she didn't look back. The black and tan hound was only a few feet away from her, snarling viciously and baring his fangs.

Joy planted her feet firmly and took a swing at the hound. The hoe handle hit him in the mouth, but Joy didn't have time to see what damage she had done, because the blue-speckled hound was closing in, too.

"Hit him, Joy!" her father shouted as he came running from the barn. He grabbed a rake and ran toward her. "Don't let him get to Snowball! Hit him if you can!"

Snowball was behind Joy and the hound was in front of her. She didn't move until the hound came very close. Then she struck overhanded with a blow that sent the dog reeling. She drew her hoe handle back and stood ready to strike again if either hound attacked. When Don got there to help her, the black and tan hound had already slipped away with his tail between his legs. The blue-speckled hound staggered to his feet and slunk off, too.

"You saved him again!" her father said proudly. "Those dogs would've torn him to pieces if you hadn't stopped them! How did you have the courage to do it, Joy?"

"I don't know," she said. "I just knew I couldn't let them kill Snowball!"

"I told you he'd come back!" Don said. "They can't

156

keep him in that game reserve! He knows where he belongs and he's come home to stay!"

"But Daddy, what about John Wilburn?" Joy asked. "As soon as he finds out that Snowball has come back home, he'll just come and take him away again!"

"I've already thought about that. I'm going to go see Oscar Timmons again tomorrow. I think he may be able to help us now..."

"But how, Daddy?" Joy interrupted.

"Let me explain, Joy. The state game laws are meant to protect wildlife. Since an albino deer is such a rare animal, the state should be especially interested in protecting him. We have proof now that Snowball would be safer here with us than anywhere else, so..."

"So Snowball will stay here with us!" Joy interrupted again. She put her arm around Snowball's neck and said, "Don't worry—everything's going to be all right now!"

"Yes, everything is going to be all right," Don said softly as he watched Joy and Snowball walk side by side down the path toward Tomorrowland.

About the Author

Jesse Hilton Stuart
Educator and Author
(1906-1984)

The late Poet Laureate of Kentucky, Jesse Hilton Stuart, published 2,000 poems, 460 short stories, and more than 60 books. In addition to being one of Appalachia's best known and most anthologized authors, his works have been translated into many foreign languages.

Yet his contributions are more than literary. During his life, this charismatic educator and author served as a leader for the people of his mountain homeland and as a spokesman for values like hard work, respect for the land, belief in education, devotion to country, and love of family. His life and works still attract hundreds of tourists to eastern Kentucky every year.

Jesse Stuart was born on August 8, 1906, in northeastern Kentucky's Greenup County, where his parents, Mitchell and Martha (Hilton) Stuart, were impoverished tenant farmers. From his father, Stuart learned to love and respect the land.

He later became a far-sighted conservationist—donating over 700 acres of his land in W-Hollow to the Kentucky Nature Preserves System in 1980.

Mitchell Stuart could neither read nor write, and Martha had only a second-grade education, but they taught their two sons and three daughters to value education. Jesse graduated from Greenup High School in 1926 and from Lincoln Memorial University in Harrogate, Tennessee, in 1929. He then returned to Greenup County to teach.

By the end of the 1930s, Stuart had served as a teacher in Greenup County's one-room schools and as high school principal and county school superintendent. These experiences served as the basis for his autobiographical book, *The Thread That Runs So True* (1949), hailed by the president of the National Education Association as the finest book on education in fifty years. The book became a road map for educational reform in Kentucky. By the time it appeared, Stuart had left

Mitchell and Martha Stuart

160

the classroom to devote his time to lecturing and writing. He returned to public education as a high school principal in 1956-57, a story told in *Mr. Gallion's School* (1967). He later taught at the University of Nevada in Reno in the 1958 summer term and served on the faculty of the American University of Cairo in 1960-61.

Stuart began writing stories and poems about Appalachia in high school and college. During a year of graduate study at Vanderbilt University in 1931-32, Donald Davidson, one of his professors, encouraged him to continue writing. Following the private publication of Stuart's poetry collection *Harvest of Youth* in 1930, *Man with Bull-Tongue Plow* appeared in 1934 andwas widely praised. Mark Van Doren, for instance, likened Stuart to the eighteen-century Scotish poet Robert Burns.

Stuart began his autobiographical, *Beyond Dark Hills*, while he was at Vanderbilt. Published in 1938, it inspired readers to follow Stuart's example of overcoming great obstacles to obtain an education. His first novel, *Trees of Heaven*, appeared in 1940, followed by short story collections H*ead o' W-Hollow* (1936) and *Men of the Mountains* (1941). More than a dozen other short story collections were published in Stuart's lifetime.

He was also a widely-read novelist, and critics such as J. Donald Adams ranked Stuart as a first-class local colorist. His first novel, *Trees of Heaven* appeared in 1940, followed by *Taps for Private Tussie* (1943), an award-winning satire on New Deal relief and its effect on Appalachia's self-reliance.

Taps catapulted Stuart to success, but the critical reaction was mixed. Some saw it as nothing more than a comical, almost stereotyped story of poor, lazy mountaineers on relief, while others explained that Stuart wrote for a popular rather than a high brow audience.

Stuart was a successful poet. His ten volumes of verse include *Album of Destiny* (1944) and *Kentucky Is My Land* (1952). He was designated as the Poet Laureate of Kentucky in 1954 and was made a fellow of the Academy of American Poets in 1961. Stuart also wrote a number of books for children that are still highly regarded and much in use today. *The Beatinest Boy* (1953) and *A Penny's Worth of Character* (1954) are two of his eight junior novels for readers in grades 3-7. *Hie to the Hunters*, a novel published in 1950, is a celebration of rural life that has been especially popular with readers in grades 7-12.

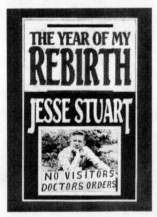

Stuart suffered a major heart attack in 1954. During his convalescence, he wrote daily journals that were the basis for *The Year of My Rebirth* (1956), a book recording his rediscovery of the joy of life. He later became an active spokesman for the American Heart Association.

Throughout his adult life, Stuart received numerous honors as a writer and educator. In 1944, the University of Kentucky awarded him his first of many honorary doctorates. October 15, 1955 was proclaimed "Jesse Stuart Day" by the Governor of Kentucky and a bust of Stuart, which is still standing, was unveiled on the Greenup County Courthouse lawn. In 1958, he was featured on *This Is Your Life*, a popular television show. In 1972, the lodge at Greenbo Lake State Resort Park was named the Jesse Stuart Lodge. In 1981, he received Kentucky's Distinguished Service Medallion.

In 1978, Stuart was disabled by a stroke. In May 1982, he suffered another stroke which rendered him comatose until he died on February 17, 1984. He is buried in Plum Grove Cemetery in Greenup County, close to W-Hollow, the little Appalachian valley that was the setting for many of his works.

Jesse Stuart Foundation

We at the Jesse Stuart Foundation (JSF) are deeply committed to our dual mission of preserving the human and literary legacy of Jesse Stuart while fostering appreciation of the Appalachian way of life through our book publishing and other activities. The JSF has reprinted many of Stuart's out-of-print books along with other books that focus on Kentucky and Appalachia. The Foundation promotes a number of cultural and educational programs and encourages the study of Jesse Stuart's works and related regional materials. Our primary purpose is to produce books which supplement the educational system at all levels.

We have thousands of books in stock and we want to make them accessible to teachers and librarians, as well as general readers. We also promote Stuart's legacy through videotapes, dramas, readings, and other presentations for

Jesse Stuart Foundation headquarters in Ashland, Kentucky.

school and civic groups, and an annual Jesse Stuart Weekend at Greenbo Lake State Resort Park. We are proud of the fact that we have become a significant regional press and bookseller and a major source of books for writers, historians, educators, collectors and readers of all ages.

For more information, contact:
Jesse Stuart Foundation
1645 Winchester Avenue
Ashland, KY 41105
(606) 326-1667

Internet Address:
jsfbooks.com
E-mail Address:
jsf@jsfbooks.com